LETTERS
FOR A SPY

Alice Chetwynd Ley

SAPERE
BOOKS

LETTERS
FOR A SPY

Published by Sapere Books.

11 Bank Chambers, Hornsey, London, N8 7NN,
United Kingdom

saperebooks.com

ISBN: 978-1-912546-93-0

To E.M. Allcott,
who always enjoyed a spy story.

'Five and twenty ponies
Trotting through the dark—
Brandy for the Parson,
'Baccy for the Clerk;
Laces for a lady, letters for a spy.
And watch the wall, my darling, while the Gen'lemen go by!'
RUDYARD KIPLING

Chapter I: The Travellers

He was decidedly the most interesting looking man in the ballroom, though not perhaps the most handsome. There was tacit agreement on this point among the young ladies who, owing to a temporary lack of partners, were obliged for the moment to sit watching the dancers. Dark brown hair carelessly swept back from a strong face, a devil-may-care smile and yet an indefinable air of decision and authority — there was scarcely one of the pretty wallflowers on the gilt chairs who did not envy the unknown gentleman's blonde partner.

'Who is he?' whispered one of these to her companion, a very fashionable young lady with a vandyked hem to her gown and two ostrich plumes in her hair.

'Oh, how should I know, dearest Marianne?' replied the other, her eyes firmly fixed on another gentleman, who had paid her a great deal of attention when last they met. 'I can't know every Tom, Dick and Harry; but this much I can say, he is no one of any particular importance, or we should have been sure to be introduced to him straight away.'

The first young lady realised that this was true, and felt sorry for it. Mama would never bother to seek an introduction for her daughter to a gentleman who was of no particular importance, no matter how many hints might be thrown at her. She sighed, consoling herself with the thought that most likely the unknown gentleman was already married.

As it happened, he was not. Marriage did not fit into his particular mode of life, which was roving and adventurous, and required the exercise of all his wits. Only once had he thought seriously of marriage. Whenever he recalled this occasion, he smiled wryly: it had not been a success. But he was not a man to brood over past failures, especially not when the present offered him scores of pretty girls to dance with and a good supper to follow. He could look back, if he chose, on occasions when he had been forced to dine meagrely and sleep rough. He smiled down at his golden-haired partner as he reflected that for a few weeks, at least, he would be able to enjoy the pleasures of civilisation.

His rejoicing came too soon. When the dance was ended, a footman brought him a note. It was unobtrusively given and taken, and was read in the privacy of the cloakroom.

'Hell and damnation!' said the gentleman, softly, when he had read the curt message. Then he gathered up his belongings, made a brief and fictitious excuse to his host, and left.

A carriage conveyed him expeditiously to a house in Piccadilly. He was shown into a quiet, elegant room on the ground floor, and immediately greeted by a man who was already waiting there.

'You wasted no time, I see. I'm glad of it, for there is none to waste. You leave for Sussex at once, my friend.'

The visitor raised his dark eyebrows. 'And my furlough, which I believe you yourself said I had earned?'

'So you had, b'God. You did splendidly over that Tilsit affair — splendidly. The present crisis touches that. Let me explain it to you over a glass of wine — but we must be brief, my dear fellow, for speed is of the essence.'

'As you will, sir,' replied the young man, with a shrug, as the other poured some wine and handed it to him. 'But I don't mind confessing I had other plans for the immediate future. I was at a ball when you summoned me, as you will see from my attire.'

'You've a good leg,' approved his host, smiling. 'Well, if your plans wear muslin, as I don't doubt they do, they'll be here to greet you on your return. And now to business. The gist of it is this…'

He spoke rapidly for ten minutes, interrupted only occasionally by a brief question from his visitor, very much to the point. At the end of it, the dark young man stood up and set down his glass.

'Two females, journeying from London to the White Hart Inn at Lewes — one youngish, one in middle years. And you can furnish me with no description of either?'

The elder man shook his head. 'The only man who could have done that is dead. But it's the younger woman you'll need to watch — the other is nothing.'

'And there is some connection with a place called Crowle, a hamlet on the South Coast not far from East Bourne? But there is no clue as to what exactly this connection may be?'

A rueful shrug greeted this question. 'I wish you luck, my boy.'

'And, b'God, I'll need it!' replied the other with a short laugh, as he turned to go. 'If ever in all my life I started off on such a wild goose chase!'

The handsome maroon and black coach bearing the Royal arms on its panels was just about to move off from the inn yard. The guard, resplendent in scarlet and blue uniform and with a gilt band round his hat, had planted his feet firmly on the locked mail box and raised the post horn to his lips, ready to blow a cheery call as the coach swung under the archway into the cobbled London street.

But the notes never sounded. Even as he took a deep breath in preparation, a female figure hurtled out of the inn door, and almost flung herself at the departing coach. The coachman tightened the reins, the horses plunged then came to a standstill. The guard's yard of tin was jerked from his hand, falling with a clatter to the ground. Swearing volubly, he dived after it.

'Well, ma'am?' he demanded loudly, bearing down on the newcomer with a belligerent glare. 'What's the meanin' o' this eh? Don't ye know the mail runs strict to time? eh? Eight o'clock from the General Post Office in Lombard Street is our time, ma'am, and five minutes it takes me to reach there. And 'ere it is five to eight this very minute, and ye no doubt expectin' as I shall hold up the coach another five or ten minutes to let ye aboard.'

'Oh!' replied the newcomer, breathlessly, 'Oh, yes — if you will be so good! I do apologise — I was unavoidably detained.'

'Unavoidably detained,' repeated the guard, with heavy irony — 'Well, I must try that some time with the superintendent. Not that I think it'd be much use. Very suspicious man, our superintendent is, ma'am, ye'd never credit.'

All the time he was talking, he had been opening the coach door and letting down the steps. He handed the tardy passenger up thrusting her unceremoniously inside and throwing after her the small carpet-bag which she had set down on the ground before mounting the steps.

'Your luggage can stay inside with ye,' he said brusquely. 'We're taking up no more passengers this trip, so there'll be plenty o' room with only the three of ye inside. *Now* can we get started?'

The passenger ignored this sally, concentrating on settling herself more comfortably into her seat and placing her carpetbag beside her.

The other two passengers in the coach, both ladies, eyed her with well-bred caution. It was unusual to find a lady travelling unaccompanied. A governess might sometimes be obliged to do so, but she would be more likely to choose the stage rather than the more expensive Mail coach. This lady did not look at all like a governess. She had an air of assurance that would surely be a poor recommendation to most prospective employers, and her clothes, though not ostentatious, were good. Elizabeth Thorne, the younger of the other two passengers, found herself speculating about the newcomer's age. She might have been anything between twenty-five and forty; it was difficult to say. Evidently she did not reciprocate the interest shown in her by her fellow-travellers; for after a cursory glance, she turned her head away to stare out of the window.

Elizabeth, too, looked away, picking up the book which lay in her lap.

'I am glad you thought of this, Margaret,' she remarked to her companion. 'A guide book is just the very thing we shall require.'

'It's rather an old one, I'm afraid,' replied Miss Ellis. 'And it's incomplete, because there should be a map in the pocket at the back, and it seems to be missing. The book belonged to my father, and came to me with some other of his things when he died. He was a very methodical man, so I can only suppose that the map was lost in transit. However, I have seen similar copies on sale in several bookshops, so it should not prove too difficult to buy another, if you wish. This one will serve for the moment, perhaps.'

'Oh, yes. It might even be more amusing,' said Elizabeth, turning the charm of her gentle smile on her friend, 'to try and do our exploring without the aid of a map.'

'No doubt we shall have enough to do at first setting the house to rights,' replied the more practical Margaret.

'The housekeeper, Mrs. Wilmot, seemed to have everything in order when we first came down to look over it,' demurred Elizabeth.

'That may be. But there are bound to be changes you wish to make.'

Elizabeth shook her head. 'Not if everything is running smoothly. As far as possible, I intend to allow the staff to carry on exactly as they did when my uncle was alive. We shall all be more comfortable in that way. Although I shall like having an establishment of my own at last, Margaret, I don't mean to let it take up so much of my time that I haven't any left over for the things I most want to do. You know what they are. I would like to go out a great deal in the fresh air, and explore that part of Sussex, whenever the weather is suitable. And when it is not, why, then I can go on with my writing.'

She said the last sentence with a slightly self-conscious air which had nothing, as Miss Ellis knew, to do with conceit.

'You will certainly be able to work more at that than you have done in your sister's home,' agreed Miss Ellis, dryly. 'Poor Anne! She doesn't really approve of it, you know.'

'I can't imagine why not. Writing is a perfectly proper occupation for a gentlewoman. Of course, it is more usual to copy out elegant extracts, or else keep a journal; but there can be no harm in your making up little stories, if it gives you more pleasure. After all it isn't as if you meant to publish them.'

'Don't I?' asked Elizabeth, a little wistfully. 'No, I suppose you are right. But even if I did, Margaret, what possible harm could there be?'

'My dear Elizabeth! You can't be serious!'

'I know — you will say no lady would do such a thing,' said Elizabeth, laughing. 'But what about Fanny Burney and Mrs. Radcliffe? And there was that delightful lady we met in Bath last year, a Miss Austen, if you remember. I was told by our hostess on that occasion — as a great secret — that Miss Austen has written several novels and they have been sent to a publisher, but so far he has not printed any of them. I am sure he's making a great mistake, for anyone who can be so entertaining a companion as Miss Jane Austen must be able to write a simply splendid book.'

'Well, so you are an entertaining companion my dear, if that is the only qualification needed for success as a writer.'

'Entertaining to you, perhaps. But you are prejudiced. I'm afraid Anne often finds me an irritation to the nerves.'

Miss Ellis gave the nearest thing to a snort that she could ever allow herself. 'The shoe ought to be on the other foot,' she said, with the Yorkshire forthrightness that still showed through on occasions, although she had spent twenty-five years now in the South of England, where manners were milder. 'You could be pardoned for being irritated by *Anne*, I am sure. She had taken advantage of your good nature ever since the unfortunate death of your parents left you in the guardianship of your elder brother, Mr. Edward.'

'We were so much alone,' said Elizabeth, gently. 'And you know we were not altogether happy in my brother's house. Edward, of course, meant to be kind, but unfortunately he married a difficult woman. I suppose there's something to be said on her side, though. It can't be agreeable to have two girls of sixteen and nineteen thrust on you when you have been married only a few years.'

'You always find something to say in defence of everyone,' said Miss Ellis, glancing indulgently at the young woman who had once been her pupil.

'Isn't it tiresome of me? But I suppose a novelist — or an aspiring one, anyway — has to see both sides of a question, and try to understand contrasting points of view. But I do think that both Anne and myself will benefit from seeing less of each other. Now that she has a husband and a young family, she no longer has need of my protection. I fear I sometimes forget that. Perhaps it was a mistake for me to have agreed to go and live with her and Philip; but they both pressed me so hard at the time, and I must confess the thought of continuing with Edward and his wife when Anne had gone, was too much. I allowed myself to be persuaded because I couldn't see anything else to do. It wasn't until my uncle left me this house in Sussex that it so much as crossed my mind to set up an establishment of my own. And even now I think Anne and Philip believe me quite mad to do so.'

'Well, it is a little unusual, perhaps, for a female of five and twenty to live alone. But it will only be for part of the year. You won't wish to stay in such an isolated spot during the winter months. I expect you will return to the Horleys for the winter?'

'I'm not certain.' Elizabeth hesitated. 'I half-promised Anne that I would, and yet — I don't wish to plan too far ahead at present. We're only just into July, and I hope to be fixed at Crowle Manor at least until the end of September. Time enough to decide then.'

As she spoke, she allowed her glance to wander idly towards their fellow-traveller. A certain stiffening in the other woman's attitude, a sudden, alert look which she directed at Elizabeth and withdrew at once when she saw she was under observation, made Elizabeth wonder.

Up to now, Elizabeth and Miss Ellis had been talking together in low tones, their conversation amply covered by the clopping of hoofs and jingling of harness from their own coach and from passing vehicles. But the words which Elizabeth spoke as she looked towards the third passenger in the coach must have been audible. What else could have caused that sudden, unmistakable awareness on the lady's part?

Elizabeth frowned and fell silent, thinking over what she had said. As far as she could see, there could be nothing in it to draw the attention of a complete stranger. Even an active imagination like her own could not suppose that her plans for the rest of the summer could be of the slightest interest to the lady in the opposite seat. Why should she care that a female whom she had never met before was to spend the next few months at Crowle Manor? Elizabeth puzzled. Yet something *had* drawn her attention, some word —

Crowle Manor! Of course, that would be it, thought Elizabeth triumphantly. People reacted in just that way when they heard a name that was familiar to them. Perhaps the unknown female lived in that part of Sussex. She might even know the house well; perhaps Uncle Giles may have been a friend either of herself or her family. It so, what an extraordinary coincidence, reflected Elizabeth; and how full of coincidences life was after all. She sighed; what a pity that the conventions forbade her from striking up an acquaintance with this lady, and putting her surmises to the test.

It would have been interesting to talk to someone who had known Uncle Giles really well. He was a man who had been least known by his own family. Giles Thorne had been a rover all his life, travelling widely in every accessible, and not so accessible, part of the globe. It was fortunate that he had never married, for at intervals his wife and family would have been forced to endure absences of several years. He had bought the house in Sussex on the twin recommendations that it was isolated, so that he need never bother with neighbours; and that it was close to the coast, so that he could put ashore or board ship again as his fancy happened to dictate, with the least possible delay. When ashore, he had seldom bothered to visit his relatives, and had never issued any invitation to them to stay at Crowle Manor.

Elizabeth remembered him at her parents' funeral, a strange, bronzed figure wearing a beard in an age when fashion decreed that men should be clean-shaven. She recalled, too, how his glance had travelled shrewdly over the mourners, summing them up. He had not stayed long afterwards, but before he left, he had sought her out in private, and a strange brusque conversation ensued.

'You're not like the rest of 'em,' he had said, eyeing the slim figure in deep mourning and noticing the reddish tints in the soft brown hair. 'More spirit — more like myself. I'd hazard a guess that you'll sacrifice yourself to that whey-faced miss, though.'

'Do you refer to my dear sister Anne, sir?' Elizabeth asked coldly, an angry expression suddenly giving firmness to a face softened by suffering.

'No need to get in your high ropes,' he had said, patting her cheek. 'Ay, you love her dearly, I can see. You're a female capable of loyal affection, and such a one as a man might be proud to take for wife — though for my own part, I'll continue to steer clear of even the best of 'em. I prefer freedom to captivity, any day. So you're to live with your brother, Edward and that shrew of a wife of his, are you?'

Elizabeth nodded.

'Well, you'll catch cold at that,' he had continued with a laugh. 'Oh, ay, you've a nice sense of gratitude and duty, I dare say, and know how to keep a still tongue in your cheek better than most of your sex. But there's something of me there, child, and one day it'll break loose and consign all your prim and proper relations to the devil. When that day comes there's a home for you down at Crowle Manor, if some ardent knight hasn't made off with you on his charger long before then. Remember what I say, child, and don't be afraid to come to me.'

With another pat and an airy nod, he had left her, and less than an hour later he had quitted the house of mourning.

She had neither seen nor heard of him again until the news of his death came to them six months ago. When his affairs were settled, her relations had expressed great surprise that he should have bequeathed the house in Sussex to Elizabeth; but remembering their conversation of six years before Elizabeth herself was not so very surprised.

They had all taken it for granted that she would sell Crowle Manor. Perhaps she had surprised herself as much as the others by deciding on a sudden impulse that she would keep the house, and live in it at any rate for a part of the year. She knew from what her uncle had told them that his household arrangements were highly satisfactory. His will requested that the same housekeeper who had been with him for fifteen years should be kept on, together with her husband. Edward Thorne had insisted that if Elizabeth really was serious about meaning to live in the place, the family should go down there and see whether they themselves thought the domestic arrangements suitable. She found herself resenting for the first time this brotherly supervision of her affairs, but reminded herself that after all it was prompted by affection. A few days' stay convinced everyone that the house was run to perfection, although Anne took an instant dislike to it and stated emphatically that she could not imagine how Elizabeth could ever bring herself to live there. She tried earnestly to persuade her sister against the scheme.

'You will not like it, dearest. It is so remote, and — and secretive, somehow, with that wooded hill behind it, closing it in. I declare, it gives me the shivers! Do not ask me to stay there with you, for I cannot! I hope you will think better of the notion and sell the house, so that we may all go on comfortably together at home as we have been doing. Philip thinks so, too, do you not, my love?'

Her husband had replied suitably, but stressed the fact that Elizabeth must be allowed to decide for herself. Something in his tone told his perceptive sister-in-law that fond though he was of her, he might not be sorry to have his wife to himself for a longer period than those occasioned by Elizabeth's periodic short visits to friends and relatives in other parts of the country. It was enough to make her stand firm against all Anne's persuasions.

Miss Ellis, once their governess but now retired from the profession, offered herself as a companion to whom even Anne could not raise the smallest objection. Margaret Ellis had a cousin in East Bourne whom she had long promised to visit, and East Bourne lay only a few miles to the east of Crowle. Miss Ellis could accompany Elizabeth on the journey, see her former pupil safely settled at Crowle Manor, and thereafter divide her time between her cousin, Mrs. Hobson, and Elizabeth. It was an arrangement that suited all parties.

Margaret Ellis was a sensible woman and an agreeable companion, and Elizabeth had turned to her often since the death of her own mother. A steady friendship had grown up between them, despite the disparity in age. In a way, both of them had a sense now of setting out on an adventure; although this feeling was naturally stronger in Elizabeth, who was breaking away at last from a life which she had scarcely realised had grown tedious.

Perhaps if they could have known the extent of the adventure which lay before them, both ladies would have stopped the coach at once and taken the first available vehicle back to London. The future being mercifully hidden, they sat relaxed in their places, chatting and falling silent by turns, while outside the shadows lengthened as the Mail coach sped steadily onwards through the countryside.

Chapter II: Incident on the Road

It had been dark for some time when they reached East Grinstead, where they halted for a quarter of an hour, one of the longest stops permitted to the Mail. Elizabeth and Miss Ellis descended from the coach to stretch their cramped limbs, but the third passenger remained in her place and appeared to be dozing.

In spite of the lateness of the hour, the landlord of the inn came out to press refreshments on them, and they were glad to accept a cup of coffee; but it arrived so scalding hot that they could not finish it before being obliged to resume their seats. It revived them, however, sufficiently to start them talking again when they were back in the coach. Out of consideration for the lady in the opposite seat, they tried to keep their voices lowered.

'We shan't reach Lewes until six o'clock,' remarked Elizabeth. 'It will scarcely be worth going to bed then. Shall we climb up to the castle, and watch the town waking?'

Miss Ellis shuddered. 'No such thing! I shall need a few hours on my bed before I can face any exercise, you may depend. I suggest we lie down for a while, then take a late breakfast, and look round the town later in the day. We will retire early the following night, so that we have a good night's rest to fortify us for the remainder of our journey to Crowle — that is, if you mean to go on to Crowle on Wednesday morning.'

'Oh, Margaret! I fear you've no romance in your soul!' exclaimed Elizabeth, laughing.

'Whatever should I do with it if I had? Romance is all very well for a female of your years, but at my time of life, it would be a sore trial.'

'Sometimes I think it's a sore trial at any time of life,' returned Elizabeth, with a little sigh.

Miss Ellis shot a keen glance at her, but the lamps of the coach did little to relieve the gloom of the interior, so that it was impossible to see her expression.

'Very likely, my dear.'

'However that may be,' continued Elizabeth, in a lighter tone, 'I'm sure you're right, as usual. It will be more sensible to do as you suggest, and go straight to bed when we arrive. And I shall leave for Crowle Manor early on Wednesday — we'll finish our journey by post chaise, if there's one to be had.'

'Oh, there's sure to be. There are two other good inns in the town, always supposing the "White Hart" cannot supply our needs, which I think very unlikely. I have never stayed there myself, but I've heard good accounts of the inn. I collect that we may rely on finding the beds clean and aired, and the food wholesome.'

'Talking of food reminds me that I am feeling hungry. I think we shall require a light meal of some kind before we retire, when we do arrive in Lewes.'

A slight movement from the other side of the coach told Elizabeth that the lady on the opposite side was awake now, even if she had been sleeping formerly, which was not certain. Margaret noticed it, too, and whispered that perhaps their chattering had disturbed her. Any compunction they felt turned out to be unnecessary, for five minutes later the coach reached a tollgate, and the guard roused the gatekeeper with a blast on the yard of tin which could well have wakened a whole village. At the next stage, the horsekeepers were also asleep, instead of standing in the road waiting with a fresh team all ready for harnessing to the coach as was the rule. Another fierce blast on the horn brought them tumbling out of the hay loft, rubbing the sleep from their eyes. To the accompaniment of a sound scolding from the irate guard, they led out fresh horses and fumblingly made the necessary change, yawning loudly as they took the old team back to the stables. Elizabeth, who was sitting on the offside of the coach, let down the window and leaned out to watch the operation by the wan glow of the lights which hung on either side of their vehicle.

After this diversion, she found herself succumbing to the soporific influence of the swaying motion of the coach and the regular clopping of hoofs in the otherwise silent night. Conversation flagged; she leaned her head back, closing her eyes.

It seemed a long time later that she came to with a jerk that almost threw her out of her seat. She clutched hurriedly at the strap for support, and saw that the others were in the same predicament. The carpet-bag belonging to the lady in the opposite corner fell from its place beside her on to Miss Ellis's legs. At the same moment *A Tour of Sussex* also slid from the seat to the floor.

'What in the name of heaven has happened?'

It was the third passenger who spoke, her tone agitated.

'The driver pulled up suddenly for some reason,' answered Margaret in her usual calm way. 'Perhaps someone — or an animal, possibly — ran into the road. I don't think there's any cause for alarm.' She stopped and lifted the carpet-bag, holding it out to its owner. 'I trust you had nothing breakable in your baggage, Ma'am.'

'Oh, no — thank you,' replied the other, taking the bag and replacing it beside her. 'We don't seem to be going on, though, do we? And I can hear voices — several others beside those of the coachman and guard, I fancy. I'll take a look outside.'

She lowered the window and leaned out, but presently drew her head in again — 'It's of no use,' she said in a disappointed tone. 'They seem to be on *that* side, whoever they are.' She nodded her head in the direction of Elizabeth's window.

Partly to oblige their uneasy companion and partly to satisfy her own curiosity, Elizabeth lowered her window and leaned out to see what was happening. A group of men stood in the road close beside the horses; among them she quickly identified the driver and guard of the coach, as the latter was holding the small portable lantern which he normally used for reading the labels on the mail bags. Some kind of argument seemed to be in progress; she listened intently for a while without being able to hear very much of what was said.

Presently she turned her head to pass on to the others in the coach the little she had succeeded in overhearing.

'There are two other men out there with our driver and guard,' she whispered. 'I can't hear everything they say, but there's something about making a search, I think.'

'A search?' The third passenger's tone was unexpectedly sharp. 'Of the coach, do you mean? Are you certain of that?'

'No, but I'll listen again,' replied Elizabeth, leaning out of the window once more.

'Possibly these are Customs men,' remarked Margaret. 'I've been told that at times they do stop coaches looking for contraband.'

'But surely that would only be coaches coming from the coast, and not those from London,' objected the other. 'These must be something else — it can't be that. There is some other reason.'

Her tone was brusque, and Margaret took exception to it. She might have made a crushing reply, but at that moment Elizabeth turned to appeal for silence so that she could better hear what was passing outside. Miss Ellis rose from her seat, turning her back on the third passenger and joining Elizabeth at the window, where she, too, strained her ears to try and follow the conversation.

In a few moments it ceased, and the group of men broke up, the coachman remaining at the horses' heads while the guard accompanied the others to the back of the coach, where the mail box was situated.

'Is anything amiss, guard?' asked Elizabeth, as they drew level with the window. 'Shall we be long delayed?'

'No longer than it takes to look into the mail box, ma'am,' replied one of the other men, in a hearty official voice, 'and to make sure as it's no more than letters our friend here's a-carrying.'

'And I tell you,' replied the guard, belligerently, 'you'll find no parcels o' game nor fish in *my* mail box. I'm not such a danged fool as to lose a good job with regular pay and uniform found, for the sake o' making a paltry sum on the side a-carrying illegal parcels.'

'No doubt, no doubt,' said the other jocularly — 'Still, we'll just open up and see for ourselves, if you don't mind, Mr. Harris.'

'Wasting my time, that's what it is,' snorted Mr. Harris. 'And me on the King's business, don't forget.'

'We're all on the King's business, my good man,' was the retort as the three moved on. 'And don't *you* forget *that!*'

'What is it all about?' asked the third passenger sharply, as Margaret and Elizabeth resumed their seats. 'Do they mean to search in here?'

'No, they seem to suspect the guard of carrying illicit parcels. Perhaps he has been known to do so before, or possibly it may be a periodic routine inspection. If he is telling the truth — he swears he has nothing — we should not be long delayed,' replied Elizabeth.

'Oh!' The stranger drew in a sharp breath. 'Is that all? You are certain? There can be no mistake?'

Her insistence was only just on the right side of civility. Elizabeth looked at her with a lively curiosity which remained unsatisfied, as it was impossible to read anyone's expression in that dim light.

'Oh, yes.' Elizabeth's reply was cold. 'They spoke only of searching the mail box at the back of the coach.'

'It's tiresome. One does not expect delays when travelling by Mail,' returned the stranger, in a peevish tone.

'I fancy all is settled,' said Margaret Ellis, a few moments later, as they heard the lid of the mail box shut with an emphatic slam. 'Either our guard is vindicated, or else he has been found out. In either case, we should be on our way again soon.'

Sure enough, in a few moments the coach started to move forward, slowly at first, and then with gathering speed. The stranger offered no further comment, but sat quietly in her corner. Elizabeth would have liked to discover what Margaret thought of their neighbour's recent behaviour, but dared not discuss it for fear of being overheard. It seemed to her that the stranger's abrupt questions had indicated some underlying uneasiness other than a natural concern at being delayed. Would it have been especially unwelcome to her if the coach had been searched by Customs men? Why? Had she something to hide? Was she perhaps carrying some contraband? The notion seemed outrageous — it *was* outrageous. Elizabeth told herself with a smile that she must curb her novelist's tendency to see drama in every little incident that was at all unusual. After all, there was nothing abnormal in feeling a strong dislike of having one's baggage searched. She would have disliked it herself, and so would Margaret.

With these reflections, she fell into a light doze, and did not wake until the coach reached Lewes.

There was a scramble then to collect their belongings, while an obliging ostler held up a lantern to aid them.

'You have the guide book, I imagine,' said Margaret, as she stepped down from the coach.

Elizabeth started. 'Oh, dear, no! I thought you had it. It must be still inside. I recollect it fell on to the floor when we pulled up so suddenly.'

Turning back, she searched for the book by the light of the ostler's lantern. It certainly was not on the floor, as she saw at a glance, nor on either seat. She bent to peer underneath the seats, then hesitated a moment before politely requesting the third passenger to move over a little in case it had chanced to slide behind her feet.

The stranger seemed extremely reluctant to comply with this request; but after a second polite application on Elizabeth's side, she grudgingly moved.

Elizabeth bent down and, with a satisfied exclamation, retrieved *A Tour of Sussex* from beneath the recently vacated seat. She thanked the lady, who favoured her with a hostile glare, and rejoined Margaret, who was watching the guard hand down their luggage to one of the inn porters. 'What a disagreeable female that is!' she remarked to her friend. 'I'm not at all sorry we're parting company, are you?'

'Hush!' warned Margaret. 'She is just behind us.'

Surprised, Elizabeth turned, then stared.

Their fellow-traveller had hitherto shown no sign at all of being about to leave the coach. Yet here she was standing in the yard of the White Hart Inn, her carpet-bag beside her.

Chapter III: Face from the Past

Their travelling companion followed them into the inn, where presently they heard her asking to be conducted to the room that had previously been reserved in the name of Mrs. Wood. The landlord, with that barely concealed air of disdain common to innkeepers who perceived a lady travelling unaccompanied, handed a key to one of the servants with the brusque comment 'Number Seven.' Towards Miss Thorne and Miss Ellis he was more affable, personally conducting them to two adjoining bedrooms on the first floor near the head of the main staircase. These were numbers Two and Three, and a communicating door made it possible to pass from one room to the other without going out into the corridor. As both rooms were similar in size and equally comfortable, there was no difficulty in deciding who should occupy which; Elizabeth settled in Number Two, which was nearer to the head of the stairs.

Both ladies felt too weary to face a meal until they had rested, so a drink of warm milk was brought up to them, and they gave instructions that they were not to be disturbed until ten o'clock.

After drinking the milk in a silence punctuated by politely smothered yawns, Margaret retired to her own room and Elizabeth prepared to lie down on the bed. She first closed and shuttered the window, for it looked out on the noisy stable-yard; then, having removed her gown, she sank on to the mattress with a sigh of deep contentment, and was soon fast asleep.

She woke with a start some time later. Something had disturbed her, but at first she could not think what it had been. Perhaps a chambermaid had tapped on the door; she pushed back the coverlet, straining her ears for a repetition of the knock. It was then that she became conscious of a far more disturbing sound, and one that was close at hand. It was the faint hiss of a quickly drawn breath.

There was someone in her room.

At first, the realisation set her heart thudding with fear so that she was unable to move or cry out. She recovered in a moment. How stupid she was; of course, it would be Margaret. She raised herself on one elbow.

'Is that you, Margaret? Surely it's not ten o'clock already?'

There was no reply. Instead, she heard a quick movement, a slight thud as something solid dropped to the floor, and the sound of the door knob turning. But it was not the knob of the door leading into Margaret's room.

Fully awake now, she sat bolt upright. By the sparse light which filtered through the chinks in the shutters, she was just able to glimpse a shadowy figure gliding swiftly from the room.

It could not have been Margaret, or she would have used the communicating door. Then who in the world had it been?

In an instant she was out of bed and groping round for her dressing-gown. She found it, and flinging it hastily round her shoulders, pulled the door open and looked out into the corridor.

No one was there. She hesitated for a moment, then crept to the head of the stairs, peering down. Curious as she was to catch a glimpse of the intruder, she would not have dared to stand there had she not known that she was safely concealed from the view of anyone passing on the floor below. This was because the staircase was in two short flights divided by a half-landing from which the lower flight bent round at an angle. She saw at a glance that no one was descending the first flight. Disappointed, she decided that she could not risk going any farther in her present state of undress. She turned and covered the few yards back to her room at a run.

Once safely inside, she stood still for a moment, deep in thought. She had a distinct impression that she had seen the door of Number One, the room next to hers and immediately at the top of the stairs, quickly closing as she passed. She had gone by so hurriedly that she could have been mistaken, of course; but the impression persisted.

Could the intruder have come from Number One? It would account for such a speedy disappearance. But who in the world could it be, and what would anyone want in her room? She shook her head. It must surely have been one of the inn-servants coming in by mistake. There was no other explanation.

She sighed impatiently, and moved across to the window to fling back the shutters. It was no use trying to think of sleeping now; she felt as wide awake as though she had been asleep all night. Just before she reached the window, she stubbed her toe on some hard object lying on the floor. With a little exclamation of pain, for her feet were bare, she stooped to massage the injured toe, and found that the offending article was a book.

She picked it up. The light was too dim to see properly, but she thought it must be the guide book. She remembered placing it on the dressing-table when she had first entered the room. Whoever had been in here must have knocked it off then; and, yes, she thought suddenly, that would account for the noise which had awakened her.

She put the book down and opened the shutters, staring out for a moment on to a grey, rainswept stableyard. Then she looked again at the book; it was *A Tour of Sussex*, as she had supposed.

She sat down on the end of the bed, frowning. What could this mean! An abigail coming into a guest's bed-chamber in error would surely leave as soon as she found the room in darkness and its occupant asleep. She would not grope her way over to the dressing-table, knocking off a book in the process. Many a girl had lost her situation for less, especially when orders had been given that a guest was not to be disturbed. Yet any other explanation of the intrusion was absurd. Who would want to visit her room except Margaret, who was safely asleep next door?

It occurred to Elizabeth that it might be as well to make sure of this, and so she softly opened the communicating door between the two rooms, and poked her head inside. Sure enough, the gentle sound of rhythmic breathing came at once to her ears. Margaret was certainly asleep, and likely to remain so for some time yet, by the signs. She closed the door again, and stood for a while meditating.

It was possible, of course, that there might be a thief at the inn. The White Hart had an unimpeachable reputation according to report, but such accidents could happen even in the best circles. Why, only last year her brother-in-law, Philip Horley, had fallen a victim to a pickpocket at the Opera, of all places; and it was a common occurrence at Ranelagh and Vauxhall Gardens. All the same, there seemed to be little enough in her room to tempt a thief. She had laid out a set of brushes and combs on the dressing-table and a small pack of other toilet aids, but these were undisturbed. So, too, when she examined it, was the rest of her baggage. If there had been a thief in her room, he or she had departed empty-handed. Perhaps she had awakened too soon; the intruder had certainly left abruptly. No doubt professional inn thieves took a chance on finding valuables lying about in a room, and left quickly when the pickings were too small, as in this instance. Elizabeth wondered if she ought to mention the incident to the landlady, and decided to discuss the point with Margaret first. It would be selfish to wake her friend now, however.

She looked at the time, and saw that it was close on seven o'clock. She decided to dress and go down to the small coffee room that was reserved for residents. She felt ready for breakfast, and though she normally might have hesitated to take a meal alone in a public room, at this time of day she ought to find it private enough.

She rang the bell for some hot water, and when the maid brought it, asked if anyone had been sent up to her room previously. The girl was emphatic that the landlady had given strict orders that the ladies in rooms Two and Three were not to be disturbed on any account before ten o'clock.

'And when the Missus says somethin', she means it, Ma'am, for sure! We all know that, right enough!'

Elizabeth made no mention of her other suspicions, but dismissed the girl. She lingered over her toilet, for there would be several hours to pass before Margaret was awake and ready to join her; and in this weather there was no prospect of taking a stroll round the town to pass the time. Fortunately she had packed a few books in her portmanteau, and there was always *A Tour of Sussex* to browse through if she could not settle to a novel.

By half past seven, she felt she could wait no longer for food; her last meal had been at six o'clock the previous evening. She left her room and was about to go downstairs when she hesitated and turned back. She removed the key from the inside of her door and locked it, then put the key into her reticule. No doubt it was an unnecessary precaution, she told herself, but at least she could now be sure that no unauthorised person would be free to enter her room. Secure in this conviction, she continued on her way downstairs.

The residents' coffee room was empty except for one gentleman who was sitting alone at the far end, his head bowed over a newspaper. She hastily averted her eyes from him, choosing a seat as far away as possible, close to the door. A waiter quickly came forward to attend to her order for toast and coffee, which was promptly brought to her table.

While she ate her breakfast with appetite, her thoughts wandered to the household she had left behind in London. Anne had thought she was mad to leave its shelter for a prolonged stay in so distant and solitary a part of the country as Crowle. Perhaps she was; but suddenly she knew that it had been more than time for her to strike out for some life of her own, before she sank completely into the role of old maid that she seemed destined to play under her sister's roof. Of course, things might have turned out very differently — she herself might have been married now, watching her own children growing up around her...

Her mind drifted for a few moments along forbidden channels.

Some extra sense, which kept guard even during her fit of abstraction, warned her that she was being watched by someone. The conviction grew, recalling her sharply to the present. She looked up from her plate, glancing quickly across at the only other occupant of the room.

He had put aside his newspaper, and was staring intently at her.

Their glances met and held for a moment. The colour rose swiftly to her cheeks, and as suddenly ebbed, leaving them pale under the light tan which summer had given her.

She was looking into a face which she would have known anywhere, even though she had not set eyes on it for six long years.

The face was changed a little, as she might have expected. There was more maturity and a certain hardness there which she did not remember noticing formerly, although she could have claimed truthfully that she had once known every contour and expression. But the brown eyes had not lost their keen, shrewd look, nor the jutting chin its firmness. There could be no mistake.

It was the face of Robert Farnham, who had once asked for her hand in marriage.

Chapter IV: The Bagman

About an hour after the arrival of the Mail coach at the White Hart, another traveller reached the inn. He came in more modest fashion, on horseback, cursing the rain which had set in suddenly a few miles back. Having seen to the welfare of his horse, which was a surprisingly good animal in view of its owner's humble station in life, he entered the White Hart by the back door.

There was no one about, so he made his way to the kitchen with the certainty of one who had often been there before. He pushed open the door, surveying the homely scene before him with deep appreciation. A good fire was burning on the wide hearth, its light flickering on the gleaming china and rows of tankards ranged along the huge dresser; several sides of bacon hung from the ceiling and the savoury smells of cooking made his mouth water.

Three serving maids were in the kitchen, each busy with a task. One of them, the most buxom and handsome, was bending over a pot which simmered over the fire, and from which the savoury odours came.

The man moved quickly across the room and gave her a playful, though hearty, slap on the rear. She spun round as the other two girls began to giggle, bringing up her hand smartly to deliver a counter-attack.

'Who's that takin' liberties?' she demanded, in a shrill indignant voice. Then, recognising her assailant, she lowered the upraised hand and chuckled.

'Oh, so it's you, Jem Potts!' she went on, in a mollified tone. 'I might 'ave knowed. And what be you a-doin' here at this time o' day?'

'I couldn't wait another hour to set eyes again on the fairest wench I ever did see in all my travels,' declared Potts, with an ingratiating smile.

'That's fustian, if ye like!' snorted Nancy, who was nobody's fool. 'Why, I'll take my oath ye say that to all the wenches — and ye a married man, most like, into the bargain.' The other two girls doubled up with laughter at this sally. Potts looked put out, but only for a moment. He took off his travelling cape, and held it at arm's length for their inspection.

'I'm wet through,' he exclaimed, needlessly. 'And not a bite past my lips since I ate my dinner at three o'clock yesterday. B'aint you going to take pity on a poor benighted traveller, and let him dry out by your fire while you prepare a tasty morsel for him to eat?'

Nancy tossed her head. 'There's the fire. No one's stopping ye from getting at it. As for victuals — well —' she paused, giving the other two girls a broad wink which set them off again — 'if ye was to ask Sally here with your best company manners, there's no saying but what she might cook you a slice or two of ham and a couple of eggs.'

'Sally, my love, you heard what she said. "Of all the girls that are so smart, there's none like pretty Sally",' carolled Potts, striking an attitude with his hand on his heart. 'Ye'll not refuse me, Sally, my own?'

'Anyone'd think ye was askin' 'er to wed ye,' snorted Nancy. 'I thought it was me ye was so set on a minute since.'

This remark set the others girls off again. After they had recovered, Sally went into the larder and returned bearing a dish which contained two thick slices of ham and three eggs.

She was soon busy cooking the bagman's meal, while he pulled a chair up beside the fire, and chatted away as the steam rose from his wet clothing.

'Got many folk staying?' he asked Nancy.

'Too many,' answered Nancy. 'Full 'ouse, as usual.'

'There'll not be many come down from London today, I reckon,' he said, spreading his hands to the blaze. 'Not in this tarnation weather.'

'The day's early yet, but we've 'ad some,' grumbled Nancy. 'There's them as come off the Mail not an hour agone, an' a gennelman as come on horseback only just now. I'm not speak-in' o' ye,' she added, with a chuckle which started the other girls laughing again.

'Who came in by the Mail, then?' he asked, carelessly.

'Oh, three ladies who're staying a night or two,' replied Nancy, giving the pot a vigorous stir and turning away with the ladle in her hand.

'All from London?'

'Why don't ye ask 'em?' retorted Nancy. 'Danged if I know — or care, for that matter.'

'Anyone else here from London?' persisted the bagman, chucking her under the chin. 'What about this gentleman ye mentioned?'

Nancy pushed his hand away, and gave him a sharp glance. 'Ye're nosey, bain't ye? What's it to ye whether they're from Lunnon or no?'

He leered at her. 'Not a thing, my love. But talking keeps my mind off my stomach, which is pinching something cruel, and a cove must talk about something, now mustn't he? Besides, folks from London is more free with their blunt than folk from these parts, and I'm always open to do a bit of good business. I've some things in my pack happen these gentry might find themselves short of. So if any of the ladies might be asking for a length of ribbon, or some pins for their hair, just remember your good friend Potts carries them all, m'dear, and then you might find something there you'd take a fancy to yourself — and that goes for all of ye, my little lovebirds, for it shan't be said that Jem Potts bain't a generous man to whosoever gives him a bit of a helping hand.'

The girls crowded round him eagerly at this, demanding a sight of his pack immediately.

'So ye shall, so ye shall,' he said, giving each of them a pat. 'But only let a cove have something to eat first, for it's hard work plying a trade like mine on an empty stomach. Ye wouldn't like to see me drop to the ground like a stone for lack o' nourishment, now would ye?'

They were about to give him an honest answer to this; but fortunately they were prevented from doing so by the entrance of Mrs. Jilkes, the landlord's wife, a thin, acid-looking woman who found no difficulty in imposing discipline on the serving maids.

'Now, then,' she demanded, arms akimbo, 'what d'ye mean by skylarkin' about with the bagman, instead o' getting on with your work? Here's the Newhaven stage due in at any minute, and not a sign o' breakfast — except for what's in your frying pan, Sally,' she amended, going over to examine the contents more closely. 'Who's this for, then? Master?'

Sally stuttered nervously that the nicely browned ham and sizzling eggs were intended for Mr. Potts.

'For Mr. Potts, indeed!' sniffed the landlady, turning a fierce stare on the bagman, who hastily stood up from his stool. 'And who's Mr. Potts, I'd like to know, that he should be waited on like Quality, while more urgent matters get left undone?'

'Well, now, ma'am,' said the culprit, in a propitiatory tone, 'I'll be paying handsome for my breakfast, and I reckon my blunt's as good as the next man's, be he Quality or no.'

'That's as may be!' snapped Mrs. Jilkes. 'You'll be staying a night or two, I suppose?'

'If quite convenient, ma'am. A bed over the stables as usual is all I need, p'raps for two nights, p'raps for longer, depending how business is hereabouts. Business, ma'am,' he concluded, attempting a leer at her but changing his mind halfway through as he met her uncompromising glare, 'business is one thing that's of equal importance to both of us, eh?'

'That's one bit o' sense out o' ye, at any rate,' replied Mrs. Jilkes, tartly. 'And just remember not to take these wenches' minds off their work. The least thing'll do that, I needn't tell ye. A more useless set o' trollops I never did see — heaven send me a respectable, hard-working wench afore I go out o' my mind —' She broke off, as the strident note of a post horn sounded, followed by a clatter of wheels and hoofs from the inn yard. 'It's the stage — I'll have to go. Just see you get on with it,' she warned, as she hurried out of the kitchen.

'Here y'are, then, Mr. Potts,' said Sally, deftly transferring the contents of the frying pan to a plate which was warming before the fire. 'It's ready.'

'That's my girl,' said Potts, approvingly, carrying the plate over to a well-scrubbed table where a place had been laid for him. 'Gladden some man's heart, one day, ye will, m'dear, if ye cook like this.'

'If she don't get on with breakfast for the stage passengers, she won't gladden Ma Jilkes's heart, an' that's a fact,' remarked Nancy. 'Not but what I doubt *she's* got a heart to gladden.'

'Stone, more like!' snorted Sally. 'Anyway, it's a waste puttin' too much in front of them stage-coach folk, for they don't get time for more than a mouthful afore they've to be off again.'

'It's a hard life, travellin',' agreed Potts, with his mouth full. 'Is there a drop of ale there, Nancy, m'dear? It'd send this down a treat, it would.'

'Ay, but ye'll have to get it yourself,' said Nancy, with a jerk of her head to the large dresser which stood against the wall. 'It's over there.'

The three girls were now bustling about in a style that must have satisfied even Mrs. Jilkes, had she still been there to see it. Potts obediently went over to the dresser, lifted a tankard down from a hook and filled it with ale. He took a deep draught, sighed with satisfaction, then refilled the tankard.

'Don't forget, now,' he reminded the girls, 'tell those ladies from the Mail that the bagman's here — and the gentlemen, too — in fact, anyone at all who's stayin' in the place. Can't tell when a bit o' business may come in your way, but it won't happen if no one knows you're there, will it, now?'

'I wonder ye don't trip upstairs and try to catch a penny or two from the folk off the stage,' scoffed Nancy, as she feverishly sliced a loaf of bread.

'Pooh!' he scoffed. 'There's nothing much to be made out o' stage passengers. Have a job to raise the fare, most of 'em. Mail coach folk are better breeched, while as for the real Quality, who travel by post chay or in their own carriages—' he sighed — 'ah, there's the goose that lays the golden eggs! But a flighty goose, mind — hard to lay your hands on for the likes o' myself.'

'But surely ye're in a bigger way o' business than that?' asked Nancy with lively curiosity, while she continued to work feverishly. 'I mind ye tellin' me one time how ye took orders from shops in all the villages for twenty mile an' more hereabouts. That ought to bring ye in a tidy bit, enough to make ye snap your fingers at small pickings from a few fine ladies an' gennelmen who might be stayin' 'ere, and too bone idle to fetch what they need from the shops in the town. Leastways, that's if ye haven't been tellin' me a pack o' lies — which I wouldn't put past ye,' she added.

'No, nor me neither,' agreed Sally, as she manipulated the idleback, a device for tipping the heavy kettle so that she could pour boiling water from it without having to lift it. 'It's my belief as Mr. Potts is a bit o' a dark horse, as they say.'

'What, me?' demanded Potts, in an injured tone. 'Well, if that don't beat all! Why, you girls know me like you know your own fathers — and I've danged near been like a father to ye, what with bringin' ye pretty gee-gaws, one time an' another. That's gratitude for ye, that is!'

'As to fathers,' retorted Nancy, lifting a loaded tray from the table, 'I never 'ad one, that I knows of, so I couldn't say, I'm sure. But all the same,' she finished, as she edged her way round the door and into the passage with her burden, 'sometimes I just wonder about ye, Jem Potts. I just wonders exactly what ye are up to, I do indeed.'

Chapter V: An Affair of Yesterday

As soon as she recognised Farnham, Elizabeth quickly looked away again. Outwardly she appeared calm, though her whole body suddenly stiffened; but inwardly she was fighting a wild upsurge of emotion which threatened to overcome her completely. Before she had time to subdue it, she heard sounds of a chair being pushed back and footsteps coming purposefully towards her. Her confusion increased. He was coming over to her table; in another moment he would be standing before her, speaking to her. Dear God, how could she face him calmly, what could she find to say?

She had never been short of courage, and it did not desert her now. As the footsteps drew nearer and halted briefly by her table, she managed to raise her head, prepared to answer something if he should speak. She could not quite bring herself to look into his face at first; she noticed that his riding breeches and top boots were liberally splashed with mud, and told herself that he had recently been riding hard, in spite of the rain. She fastened on this unimportant detail in the way that people often do in times of emotional stress, hoping to restore rationality by concentrating on the trivial.

It was only a second before she looked up, but it seemed like an hour. She waited for him to speak first. What would he say to her, after all these years? What was there to say, after the way they had parted?

Her eyes met his fleetingly, and his flickered. But there was no sign of recognition in them as he passed by her without speaking, and went through the open door out into the hall.

She sat there for a long time after he had gone, without being at all conscious of her surroundings. The waiter came once to ask if she required anything further. She must have made some kind of answer, for he deftly removed the cold remains of a cup of coffee and the half-eaten toast with butter congealing on the top, afterwards leaving her alone.

At last, she stirred, discovering that she had slight cramp in one of her legs through sitting so rigidly in her chair. She looked at the clock; the hands were moving towards nine. She must have been sitting there almost an hour. Slowly she rose, and made her way upstairs to her room.

She tried the door, and was at first surprised to find it locked. The earlier events of that morning had been completely forgotten in the more recent shock she had received. Now it all came back to her; she took the key from her reticule and unlocked the door.

Margaret was standing over by the window, fully dressed and looking out at the rain beating on the cobbled yard. She turned round as Elizabeth entered.

'Oh, there you are! I thought you would have gone downstairs, but it seemed better to wait for you here. I awoke about an hour since, but did not come in immediately, for fear you should still be asleep.' She broke off, looking sharply at Elizabeth's face. 'My dear child, is anything the matter? Do you not feel well? You look as though you had seen a ghost!'

Elizabeth laughed shakily. 'No, I'm quite well. But perhaps I have seen a ghost, in a way.'

'What do you mean?' asked Miss Ellis, sharply. 'Wait while I get you my smelling-bottle.'

She was about to dart through the communicating door into her own room, but Elizabeth made a little gesture of dissent.

'No need, Margaret, thank you. I've just had something of a shock, that's all. But it's nothing that a smelling-bottle can cure.'

'What kind of shock?' demanded her friend. Then, as Elizabeth made no answer, 'Is it something you do not wish to tell me? If so, I won't pester you, my dear. But do come and sit down, for you look fagged to death.'

Elizabeth obediently sat down, and was silent for a while. Miss Ellis watched her with an anxious expression, but did not again press her to explain.

At last, Elizabeth broke the silence with a little sigh.

'No, it isn't anything I wish to keep from you, Margaret,' she said, slowly. 'After all, at the time I confided the whole to you.'

She paused. Miss Ellis waited in the patient way that had won her many a reluctant confidence in past years. It was evident that her young friend had just been through some upsetting experience; she must be allowed to recover from it in her own time.

'There,' said Elizabeth, presently, in a matter-of-fact tone that still belied her feelings, 'I am quite myself again, but it was certainly a shock. Do you know who I have just seen, Margaret? None other than Robert — Mr. Robert Farnham, I should say.'

It was obvious that the name conveyed nothing to Miss Ellis at first. She repeated it, frowning thoughtfully. In a few seconds, her brow cleared.

'Oh, of course! I recollect now! That was the gentleman whom you met when you went to stay with your aunt in Tunbridge Wells. The one who —'

'The one who made me an offer of marriage,' finished Elizabeth quietly. 'And whom I rejected.'

'It was for your sister's sake that you did so. From what you told me at the time, I know that your feelings towards him —'

Elizabeth nodded. 'Yes — I was in love with him,' she said quietly. 'But how could I leave Anne, with our parents so lately dead? She had only me to rely on, as things were at that time.'

'You could have asked him to wait. There was no need to have rejected him out of hand — but so I told you then. I must not be tedious, repeating myself.'

'I did what seemed best, and most fair to him.'

'And what about yourself? Was it fair to you?'

Elizabeth hesitated. 'I couldn't ask him to wait, for how could I know how many years it might be before I could leave Anne? At nineteen, one year seems a long time, and three or four, for ever. I did what seemed best for everyone at the time. Besides, he wouldn't wait — his nature is not a patient one.'

'And I know,' said Miss Ellis, softly, 'that you often regretted your decision, afterwards.'

'Yes. Yes, I did. But it is some years now since he was in the forefront of my thoughts. I have long since become reconciled. Possibly we should not have suited. I was very young, after all. It may have been all for the best.'

'Where did you see him? Here at the inn, one supposes, for you will scarcely have been out of doors in this weather.'

'Yes, it was here at the inn. I went into the coffee room to have some breakfast, and he was sitting there, alone.'

'What an extraordinary thing!' exclaimed Miss Ellis. 'What did he say to you? Did he make any reference to the past?'

'He said nothing.'

'Nothing?' repeated Margaret, incredulously.

'Nothing at all. I am not even sure,' said Elizabeth, doubtfully, 'that he recognised me. There was just a flicker in his eyes as though he had some doubt whether we had met before. But he gave no sign of positive recognition, and never spoke a single word.'

'Well!' Margaret paused a moment to digest this. 'And did you say anything to him — a formal greeting, perhaps, like good morning?'

'No. I was too overcome at first — and then it was so evident that he did not know me, or did not want to know me,' replied Elizabeth, a touch of colour coming to her cheeks. 'I suppose, though, I may have changed a good deal in those six years, so he could hardly be blamed for not recognising me.'

'Nonsense! You are more handsome now than you were then, perhaps, but otherwise you are very much the same. Anyone would know you,' said Margaret indignantly.

'Then perhaps he doesn't wish to renew the acquaintance. I dare say —' she hesitated, then went on in a slightly awkward tone — 'he is most likely married to someone else by now.'

Margaret was silent for a moment, then replied, 'It could well be so. In that case, it is possible that his wife is staying here with him — that is, if he is indeed putting up at the inn, and not merely passing through the town.'

Elizabeth shook her head, and shrugged helplessly. 'That I can't say, of course.'

Margaret gave her a shrewd glance. 'I dare say you will want to change your plans now. We could leave for Crowle Manor at once, if you wish.'

'I am uncertain what I want to do,' replied Elizabeth, doubtfully. 'I never like altering my arrangements unless I'm positively obliged to do so. Besides, the housekeeper is not expecting us at the Manor before tomorrow. No, Margaret,' she finished, with more firmness in her tone, 'I am not going to run away from Robert Farnham. After a long parting, we have met again, and the worst is now over. Even if Robert —

Mr. Farnham — is staying here, there's no reason why we should not be able to share the same inn for the space of one day. He means nothing to me now — nothing at all — and it's plain that he has forgotten me completely. Perhaps it's a good thing that this has happened, for it's shown me that the past is indeed over and done with. One can never go back, only forward, as you so often used to tell me when I was still your pupil.'

Miss Ellis was not quite as reassured by this speech as perhaps her one-time pupil would have liked her to be; but she was far too wise to voice any doubts. Instead, she changed the subject by saying that she was ready for some breakfast, and would order something to be brought up to her room. Elizabeth was not sorry to hear this, for in spite of her recent speech, she felt unable to face another visit to the coffee room just yet.

It was Nancy who brought up Miss Ellis's breakfast, laying it on a small table in Elizabeth's room, as she was directed.

'Very well then, girl,' said Miss Ellis, seeing that Nancy lingered for a moment when her task was done. 'Thank you — I shan't require anything more for the present.'

'If ye please, ma'am,' ventured Nancy, mindful of her promise to Jem Potts, 'I just wanted to say there's a travelling bagman downstairs, should you be wantin' any little thing in his line, ma'am.'

'I don't think so — but thank you, all the same.'

The nod of dismissal carried a hint of impatience in it, and Nancy speedily withdrew.

'I dare say these pedlars depend for quite a portion of their trade on the goodwill of inn servants,' remarked Margaret Ellis, as she approached her breakfast with enthusiasm. 'Would you care for some coffee, Elizabeth? The girl has brought two cups.'

'To be truthful, Margaret, I would, please. I did order some downstairs, but I'm afraid I allowed it to get cold.'

'That would be when you saw Mr. Farnham, I collect?'

Elizabeth nodded, accepting the cup that her companion passed over to her. Now that she had been able to talk to someone about that unexpected meeting, she was rapidly recovering from its effects.

'That reminds me, Margaret. This latest incident has quite put out of my head something else I meant to tell you, something else that was odd.'

She recounted briefly the story of finding an intruder in her bedchamber. Miss Ellis listened, almost neglecting her own coffee as she did so.

'But how extraordinary, my love!' she exclaimed, when Elizabeth had finished. 'I suppose —' she hesitated — 'I suppose you cannot have *dreamt* it? There is a time, you know, between sleeping and waking, when one can imagine the most outrageous things —'

Elizabeth shook her head. 'No, I am certain it was no dream. Besides, how else would the book have fallen suddenly to the floor? I placed it securely enough on the dressing-table, not just on the edge, that I do remember.'

'All the same,' replied Miss Ellis, doubtfully, 'a sudden bang on the floor might have dislodged it. The abigails may have been moving the furniture in the room above yours — and that may have been what wakened you in the first place. Depend on it, my dear, it was all a dream. All the same, it will do no harm to keep your door locked. I always do so when I am staying at an inn.'

Chapter VI: Special Delivery for Crowle Manor

By the time breakfast was over, the rain had stopped, and the sun appeared from behind the rapidly breaking cloud. This improvement in the weather decided the two ladies to venture for a stroll in the town, and they quickly made themselves ready for their outing.

Elizabeth hesitated for a moment as she was about to close the door of her bedroom behind her before going downstairs, and Miss Ellis looked at her questioningly.

'What is the matter? Is there something you've left behind in your room?'

'No,' replied Elizabeth, shaking her head. 'But it's just — oh, I dare say you'll think it foolish of me, Margaret, but I think I'll lock this door while I'm away. I dislike the notion of anyone poking about in my room, and I'm positive that someone was in here earlier on. Whoever it was, may come again. Anyway, I shall not feel easy in my mind if I leave the door unlocked.'

Miss Ellis was fairly certain in her own mind that her friend must have dreamt the earlier episode; but she wisely refrained from repeating this opinion. Instead, she also locked her door, remarking that there was no use in locking one without the other, as the inner communicating door would give access to Elizabeth's room.

They had concluded this precautionary measure, and were putting the keys away in their reticules, when they heard someone approaching from that end of the passage which led to the service staircase. A moment later, their recent fellow passenger, Mrs. Wood, came into view. She favoured them with a hard, curious stare as she passed, but otherwise gave them no greeting.

'Well, really!' hissed Miss Ellis, in an indignant whisper. 'She might at least have had the courtesy to bow and say good morning!'

Mrs. Wood was descending the stairs. Elizabeth gazed thoughtfully after her rigidly-held back.

'She is an odd kind of female altogether,' she replied in a low tone. 'Her behaviour in the coach was most —' She broke off, as the door of Room One opened and a gentleman emerged. He gave no more than the briefest glance in their direction before turning to go downstairs, but it was enough for Elizabeth to identify him. To her annoyance, she felt the colour rise to her face.

Miss Ellis noticed her friend's slight confusion and, being quick on the uptake, guessed almost at once what had caused it; especially as Elizabeth showed a disposition to linger outside the door of her room instead of continuing on her way to the staircase. She asked if the gentleman had been Mr. Farnham, and was answered by an embarrassed nod.

'How very odd, my dear, that he should be in the room next to yours!' Then, after a pause — 'Shall we not go down? Perhaps it would be as well to inquire of the landlord if he can supply a chaise to take us to Crowle tomorrow. If we leave it too late, they may all be booked.'

Having thus, as she hoped, given Elizabeth's thoughts a new turn, she steered her towards the stairs. Elizabeth went down slowly, hoping to avoid catching up Mr. Farnham; but when she reached the hall, she saw that he was standing there with his back to her, apparently deeply absorbed in studying a stuffed fish in a glass case which hung on the wall. Mrs. Wood, too, was standing not far away, fastening the buttons on her grey gloves. As Elizabeth and Margaret paused at the foot of the stairs, the landlord came out of the residents' coffee room and they were able to ask him about their chaise for the following morning.

'Crowle?' he repeated, loudly. 'See, that's East Bourne way, bain't it, ma'am? Yes, yes, ye can have a post chaise and no trouble at all. And what time will ye wish to be startin', ladies?'

After a little debate, they settled on nine o'clock as a suitable time. The landlord bowed, asked if there was anything further he could do for them, and, being satisfied that there was not, disappeared into the coffee room once more.

'Well, that's settled,' said Margaret, as they stepped outside the entrance door of the inn. 'Now all our arrangements are in order, and we have nothing to do but pass the time agreeably.'

On the cobbled forecourt outside, a man was standing, dressed in a shabby snuff-coloured suit with a green neckcloth knotted round his collarless shirt. He doffed a battered, greasy felt hat as the ladies approached, and drew their attention to a valise which was open at his feet, displaying a quantity of brightly coloured silks, ribbons and small items of haberdashery.

'What d'ye lack, ladies?' he cried, in the mendicant's brisk tones. 'Honest Joe Potts can supply all yer wants at a fraction what ye'll be asked by them thievin' merchants in the town.'

Elizabeth automatically halted on being addressed, though the more experienced Miss Ellis would have walked on. At that moment, Mrs. Wood walked out of the inn, and she too paused by the pedlar's pack. Seeing that he had an audience of three females, Jem Potts was quick to press his advantage. He seized some knots of cherry-coloured ribbon and thrust them into the ladies' hands.

'Here y'are then, y'r la'ships, ma'am — see, not better anywheres in Lewes — only tuppence for that length, ma'am — cost ye three or four times as much elsewhere, I'll warrant! And here's a fine muslin, only three shillings the yard — seven yards will make ye a fine gown, y'r la'ships, and all for a guinea!'

Out of the corner of her eye, Elizabeth saw that Robert Farnham had also come out of the inn and was loitering close to the group around the bagman. Hastily she dropped the knot of ribbon she was holding, and shook her head.

'No, no — I want nothing today.'

She turned away, but the bagman leaned over towards her, speaking urgently in a slightly lower tone.

'Then mayhap there'll be some other service I can do ye, ma'am — an errand, maybe? Fetchin' and carryin'? I do all manner o' that sort o' thing — now a parcel, now a letter. Ye don't chance to 'ave anything o' that nature about ye, now, that I can relieve y'r la'ship of?'

Something in his tone gave the simple words an added significance. It was this that made Elizabeth pause instead of continuing on her way to follow Margaret, who was already several paces ahead. She looked keenly into his crafty eyes for a second without speaking.

'I'll be on the road again tomorrow,' went on the bagman, watching her just as keenly. 'South to the coast, around East Bourne. Maybe ye'll have something ye'll not care to trust to the post, something too delicate to go otherwise than by hand. If ye've anything for down that way, village or hamlet, be it so small a place as Eastdean or Crowle — then I'm y'r man, m'lady.'

'Crowle?' breathed Elizabeth.

Jem Potts opened his mouth to reply, but at that moment the landlord came bustling out of the inn towards them. He addressed himself to the pedlar, his usually jovial face clouded with annoyance. 'Now, see here, Jem Potts, I can't have ye a-pestering of my guests in this way. I've told ye afore I don't hold with ye a-settin' up to sell your wares outside the front door o' my inn. A respectable house, is the White Hart, patronised by the Quality, an' I'll not have the likes o' ye lowering the tone o' the place. Has he been bothering ye, ladies?' he asked, looking round him. 'Or ye, sir?' to Mr. Farnham, who was still lingering on the outskirts of the group, apparently idly taking the air. 'Because if he has,' went on Mr. Jilkes, without waiting for an answer, 'out he goes, bag an' baggage, ye may depend, and he'll not find a bed here again in a hurry!'

'Nonsense, landlord,' snapped Mrs. Wood, before any of the others could reply. 'The man's doing no harm that I can see — in fact, I shall certainly purchase some of this ribbon. It will save me a journey to the shops.'

Mr. Jilkes looked far from pleased at this unwelcome championship of the pedlar, but knew his business better than to disagree with a customer. He adjured Potts sharply to attend to the lady's wants and thereafter to make himself scarce. He then went back into the inn, and stood glowering in the doorway to make sure that his orders were obeyed.

Elizabeth and Margaret walked away, turning into the street. For some time they were silent, then Elizabeth said, thoughtfully, 'What could that man have meant, I wonder?'

'I collect you're referring to the pedlar?'

'Yes. He looked at me in so very particular a way when he spoke of delivering parcels or letters — though I know it is a common thing for such people to undertake. But he made it sound as if —' she paused, trying to imprison in words what had only been a fleeting impression — 'as if — he and I shared some secret, somehow. And then, what was even more odd, he mentioned Crowle. Now, why should he have done that?'

'Coincidence,' replied Margaret, with a shrug.

'Perhaps so, yet there was a curious suggestion of intent — it seemed to me that he deliberately led his remarks up to a mention of Crowle.'

'The trouble is,' said Margaret, laughing, 'that you are a novelist, my dear, and are always reading into things meanings which are not there.'

Elizabeth smiled. 'I dare say you are right,' she answered, in an unconvinced tone. 'But it is certainly strange he should mention it — after all, it's such a small place, so remote from everywhere.'

'These packmen know all the small villages in their own area,' objected Miss Ellis. 'He did mention another one as well — Eastdean, I think it was. I see nothing extraordinary in that.'

'But it was his manner,' her companion insisted. 'It was so — so — conspiratorial, is the only word I can find for it. Oh, yes, I know I'm foolish —' as Margaret burst out laughing again — 'but there *was* something odd in his manner to me, say what you will.'

They walked on in silence for a few moments.

'And there's another odd thing,' continued Elizabeth, 'I meant to ask you about it at the time, but I was afraid of being overheard. It was when we were in the coach. That female, Mrs. Wood, showed most decided signs of interest when I mentioned that we were bound for Crowle Manor. Now what can there be about our visit to Crowle that causes such interest to two such different people as Mrs. Wood and the pedlar?'

'The answer to that is so plain that you must see it yourself,' replied Margaret, in a matter-of-fact tone. 'There could be nothing except what exists in your own imagination.'

'You believed I imagined that intruder in my room, too, don't you?' accused Elizabeth.

'Well, yes, love, I do,' Margaret acknowledged, apologetically. 'You always had the strongest imagination as a child. Such delightful stories you used to make up, to entertain Anne! And then there were times when you suffered from nightmares, too,' she added. 'Your gift was always a mixed blessing to you.'

'So you consider the whole chain of incidents is nothing remarkable, and that I have in fact been suffering from hallucinations?'

'Not hallucinations — oh, dear, no!' refuted Miss Ellis, hastily. 'Only you must realise, my love, that real life is not at all like the pages of a novel by Mrs. Radcliffe — and I'm sure you do, for in spite of your imagination, you have always been the most sensible, level-headed girl in the way you have acted.'

Elizabeth fell silent again until they paused before a milliner's window which displayed several attractive bonnets.

'Now, that would be the very thing to go with my new pelisse,' remarked Miss Ellis, pensively.

'What, your dark green one?' asked Elizabeth. 'Oh, no, Margaret, yellow straw would not look at all well with it, I assure you! Do you not prefer that Grecian helmet? The ribbons are in the exact shade you require.'

The lively discussion which ensued succeeded in driving all thoughts of the day's unusual events out of Elizabeth's mind for a time.

'Well, I think I shall not buy anything until I have my pelisse with me,' decided Miss Ellis, at last. 'But I tell you what I may purchase, and that is a length of muslin for my cousin

Ernestine, for I shall not like to visit her empty-handed.' She broke off, looking up and down the street, then continued, 'There is a linen draper's farther down on the opposite side, my dear. Shall we cross over?'

They had to wait a few moments to do this, in order to allow a carriage to pass. After it had gone, they crossed over and came to a halt before the linen draper's window. Elizabeth at once started to examine the lengths of material displayed there; but after a while she gradually realised that her friend's attention had wandered. Miss Ellis kept darting covert glances behind her, and once she smiled to herself, as if at some amusing thought.

'What is it, Margaret?' asked Elizabeth at last, looking round at the people passing to and fro beside them on the pavement. 'What is it you keep looking at, that seems to amuse you so much?'

Miss Ellis nudged her quickly. 'Do not look now, love, on any account, or he will be bound to think you are watching him!'

'What do you mean? Who will think —'

'Your Mr. Farnham!' whispered her friend. 'I noticed just now, when we were waiting to cross, that he was behind us — and he has just this moment crossed over on to this side! I don't think *he* will be wanting to purchase a length of muslin, do you? Oh, no —' glancing round carefully from under the brim of her bonnet — 'he has stopped at the bookshop two doors away, and is looking in the window. At least,' she added, 'he is pretending to look in the window, but in reality he is watching us — or rather, it must be you, my dear, for I can't flatter myself that he would be at all interested in looking at me. Only fancy! He must have followed us from the inn.'

'Nonsense!' replied Elizabeth, quite sharply for her. 'You must be mistaken.'

'No, indeed I am not. I never forget a face even though I have only seen it for a moment, and his is a face one would remember — a firm chin, you know, and a strong nose. Not precisely handsome, but there is something — take a peep for yourself, if you think I am mistaken, but for heaven's sake be careful, for it will not do to let him see we have noticed him.'

Elizabeth managed a fleeting glance; it was enough to tell her that Margaret was not mistaken. It was indeed Robert Farnham loitering before the window of a bookshop less than ten yards away from where they were standing. Her cheeks grew warm again.

'Do you mean to go into this shop?' she asked hurriedly.

'Why, yes, we may as well see what they have,' replied Miss Ellis, looking into the window in an undecided way.

Elizabeth seized her arm, almost dragging her into the shop, and for the next half-hour or so they were busy examining muslins of various colours and patterns. At last Miss Ellis selected one suited to her cousin's age and style, and they waited while the draper cut off the amount required and made it up into a parcel. He offered to deliver this, but Elizabeth insisted that they should return with it to the White Hart themselves. She seemed to have lost all interest in prolonging the outing.

On emerging from the shop, they both looked sharply about them; but to Elizabeth's relief there seemed to be no sign of Mr. Farnham. After they had crossed the road, however, and were walking towards the inn, she glanced behind her and caught sight of him again, sauntering along the pavement in the same direction.

They turned into the forecourt of the inn just a little way ahead of him, and had started to ascend the staircase as he entered the hall.

Neither spoke until they were standing outside the door of Elizabeth's room. Then Miss Ellis said in a whisper, 'Upon my word, it looks very much as though he has been following us! What can he mean by it, I wonder? Do you suppose that he half-recognised you when you met earlier, and has been trying to make up his mind who you are, and where you have met before?'

Elizabeth did not answer at once; she was hunting in her reticule for the key. As she bent to insert it in the lock she began to reply, but broke off on hearing a slight noise from the direction of the staircase. She glanced quickly that way, and saw Mr. Farnham standing outside the door of the next room, on the point of entering. He seemed not to notice them, for he did not glance in their direction.

Elizabeth hastily pushed open her door, and whisked Margaret and herself inside. She began to untie her bonnet with fingers which trembled slightly.

'Well!' remarked Miss Ellis. 'Say what you will, it certainly looks as though that gentleman has been deliberately dogging our footsteps! Do you think he may have had some chivalrous notion of protecting us from people such as that pedlar who tried to importune us on our way out?'

'Now who is imagining things?' asked Elizabeth, with an uncertain laugh. 'If you ask my opinion, it is that he was taking a stroll round the town just as we were; and, as it is not a large metropolis one can't wonder if our ways happened now and then to lie together.'

Miss Ellis was above all a sensible woman, but now and then she allowed herself the indulgence of a small romantic notion.

One such had entered her head as soon as Elizabeth had told her that Mr. Farnham was staying at the White Hart. She knew that six years ago these two had been deeply in love; she had witnessed the quiet, controlled agony of Elizabeth's renunciation at that time. She could not quite subdue a hope that the present unexpected meeting would lead to a renewal of the gentleman's addresses, and that she might at last see her beloved Elizabeth settled in a happy marriage. Marriage, after all, Miss Ellis acknowledged to herself with a sigh, is a more agreeable state than spinsterhood, particularly when one is only five and twenty. She judged it prudent to say no more on the subject of Mr. Farnham at present, however.

'What shall we do now?' she asked, removing her spencer and bonnet. 'It is almost noon, and I think not too soon for a light luncheon. Shall we have it served here, or would you prefer to go down to the coffee room?'

After a little hesitation, Elizabeth decided on going downstairs.

'Do you think we might go out again for a little this afternoon, Margaret?' she asked, when this point was settled. 'Or are you too tired? I would very much like to see the ruins of Lewes castle; but if you don't feel equal to it today, we can easily come here again some other time. We shall not be so very far away, after all.'

'Too tired? Nonsense! I hope I am not such a poor creature that a short stroll round the shops in a town of this size can lay me down for the rest of the day! By all means let us go. The rain is quite finished, and it will do us good to be out of doors.'

'Well, let us see what the guide book has to say about the castle,' said Elizabeth, picking *A Tour of Sussex* up from the dressing-room and rapidly turning the pages. 'Ah, here we are — Lewes castle, with an illustration of it done in 1780. It looks very Gothic, don't you think, and quite fits any mood. "Built by William de Warenne, one of the most distinguished followers of William of Normandy" — there is a great deal more about the Warenne family. It occupies —' flicking hastily over the pages — 'three or four pages. We must read that some other time, I think. Oh, yes, here we are — farther on it says that this is the only castle with two artificial mounds, and that the Barbican is very fine. I think we must certainly see it.' She broke off abruptly. 'That's strange.'

Miss Ellis looked at her inquiringly, and saw that she had turned to the back of the book and was feeling in the pocket.

'I thought you said, Margaret, that the map was missing from the back of this book. Well, you were wrong — it is here.'

'Impossible, my dear,' replied her friend, confidently. 'I examined the book carefully before I brought it, and was most disappointed to see that there was no map.'

'There's something here, at any rate,' insisted Elizabeth. 'Let's see what it is.'

She drew her hand out of the pocket, disclosing a bulky sealed package.

'Why, it's a letter! Or rather, I should say, a packet. You must have put it in here, meaning perhaps to deliver it somewhere, and forgotten about it —'

'I did no such thing!' exclaimed Miss Ellis, sharply. 'Here, let me look at it!'

Elizabeth was about to pass the packet over, when her eye fell upon the inscription in firm copperplate on the face of it. She gave a start, and looked at it again to be sure that she had read it aright.

It was directed to J. Martin, Esquire, of Crowle Manor.

Chapter VII: Mrs. Wood Buys Some Ribbon

Elizabeth stood motionless, staring at the packet. Miss Ellis stretched out an impatient hand.

'What is it? May I not see?'

Elizabeth passed the packet to her without a word, watching while she read the inscription.

'But I don't understand.' Miss Ellis raised puzzled eyes to her friend's face. 'Do you know this connection of your late uncle's?'

'Not to my knowledge. I certainly never heard the name before in my life.'

'Then what in the world is a letter directed to him doing in our possession at all?'

'I wish I knew,' answered Elizabeth, slowly. 'I suppose there's no possibility of any error, Margaret? It could not have been in the book when you brought it from home?'

'I thought I had made that point quite clear, my dear,' said Miss Ellis, in a slightly injured tone. 'You know me well enough to understand that my word can be relied upon. I am neither a careless nor a forgetful person, I believe.'

'No, no, of course not,' replied Elizabeth, placatingly. 'But it is so incredible! It can't just have been spirited into the book. Someone must have put it there — but who?'

She relapsed into thought.

'A lunatic, obviously!' exclaimed Miss Ellis. 'Who else would do such a thing? Why, there could be no certainty that it would ever be found, for one thing!'

'I must confess that puzzles me,' admitted Elizabeth, frowning. 'Even supposing that someone wished me to deliver this packet to Mr. Martin — whoever he may be — at Crowle Manor, surely it would be simpler to hand it to me personally? Simpler and more certain of success — oh!'

She broke off abruptly. Miss Ellis raised an eyebrow inquiringly.

'The pedlar, Margaret!' continued Elizabeth, in a burst of illumination. 'You recollect his words — he asked if I had a letter or anything of that nature to be delivered anywhere, and he mentioned Crowle in the same breath! Depend upon it, he knows something about this!'

Miss Ellis considered for a moment. 'But what?' she asked at last. 'He cannot have placed it in the guide book himself, or he would not have been asking you if you had anything for him to deliver. The boot is on the other foot — whoever placed the letter in the book must have wanted *you* to deliver it.'

'Perhaps that was his way of drawing my attention to the letter —'

'Scarcely a satisfactory one,' replied Miss Ellis, dryly, 'for he never mentioned the guide book, did he?'

'No. You are right. Well, then, that will not do. But all the same, I feel certain that he knows something about this packet. He spoke in too significant a tone — it would be stretching coincidence too far —'

'Perhaps so. I must take your word for what he said, as I could not quite catch it, though I did notice the rather peculiar expression on his face. Crafty, it was.'

Elizabeth agreed, and fell silent again. After a moment, she said, slowly, 'I think perhaps the person who did it must have been the one who visited my room earlier this morning. I found the guide book on the floor, remember, and supposed at the time that the intruder had brushed it off the table in passing. Supposing instead that he or she had actually been inserting the letter into the back of the book, and perhaps misjudged the distance in replacing it on the dressing-table, so that it fell on the floor and woke me up?'

'Now, really, my dear —' began Margaret.

'I know,' Elizabeth broke in with a laugh. 'You are going to say that there'd be no sense in such an action! And then we are back at the point where we started. But we can't escape the fact that someone did put this packet in the guide book, Margaret. Here it is, to prove the fact.'

'Well, it is beyond me entirely,' sighed Miss Ellis. 'However, I suppose there is one way in which we can settle this discussion. We can open the letter and see who the sender is.'

Elizabeth considered this suggestion for a moment in silence.

'Ye-es,' she said at last, doubtfully. 'But do you think we should? It is not quite the kind of thing one likes to do, even in such odd circumstances.'

'No. I agree with you, more particularly as the name and direction are written plainly enough. On reflection, Elizabeth, I think the only honourable think we can do is to take the letter with us and try to deliver it. If there should be any difficulty in doing so, then perhaps we could open it and communicate with the sender.'

They debated the point for a while longer, but eventually agreed on this course of action.

'Well, if we are to take this with us to Crowle Manor,' said Elizabeth, 'I think it will be safer to place it in my writing portfolio, rather than keep it in the guide book. It could easily get lost, you know; and although we don't know how we came by it, still I should feel responsible would not you?'

Miss Ellis agreed, and the packet was transferred to the safety of the portfolio, which was in Elizabeth's portmanteau.

'And now for heaven's sake let us forget the wretched thing!' exclaimed Elizabeth. 'I am quite ready for my luncheon, so shall we go downstairs?'

This they did; but they took the precaution of locking their doors securely behind them.

When Elizabeth and Miss Ellis walked away from the pedlar that morning, the group in the forecourt soon dispersed. Mr. Farnham lingered for a few moments watching with what appeared to be idle interest while the bagman displayed one or two of his wares to the remaining customer; then he turned away to stroll in the same direction as the two ladies.

Jem Potts was evidently uneasy, for he kept looking towards the door of the inn, where the landlord still stood in a threatening attitude.

'I'll take this ribbon,' said Mrs. Wood, when Farnham was out of earshot. 'You mentioned just now that you would deliver a letter — I believe I may have something in that way for you.'

The pedlar shot her a keen glance. 'Ye do, ma'am?'

She nodded. 'But this is not an ideal place for us to do business, with our good host looking on, and perhaps others, too. I suggest — '

She produced some coins and leant over to place them in the pedlar's hand. As she did so, she spoke a few rapid sentences in his ear. Then, stowing away the cherry-coloured ribbon in her reticule, she turned towards the inn.

Potts lost no time in packing up after she had gone. Going through the archway into the rear quarters of the inn, he mounted a ladder to his bedroom in one of the stable lofts, flung down his pack, and afterwards made his way to the kitchen.

There was no one there but Sally, who was scrubbing down the tables with an energy that suggested that Mrs. Jilkes could not be far away.

'Workin' hard, Sally, my love?' Potts greeted her facetiously.

'Ye've got eyes, 'aven't ye? What d'ye think I be doin'? Fanning meself?' replied Sally in kind.

'And where might milady Nancy, be?'

Sally jerked a wet thumb at the ceiling. 'Upstairs, helpin' with the bedchambers. Short o' staff we be, at present — works like slaves, we do, and never no thanks for it. Nothin' but black looks and mebbe a boxed ear from Missus now an' then, just for a treat, like.' She sniffed.

Potts nodded gravely. 'It's a hard life, is business o' any kind,' he agreed. 'And no one knows that better nor me. Tell me, love, what happens if one o' they guests goes out and leaves their bedchamber door locked? Can the maids get in to do the cleaning?'

'Course they can,' replied Sally, scornfully. 'There's another set o' keys, stupid, bain't there?'

'I don't know — I bain't an innkeeper,' retaliated Potts. 'Who keeps them, then?'

'Mrs. Jilkes, mostly. She hands them over to the chambermaids at cleaning times, though. Nancy's got them now.'

'Got a finger in every pie, our Nancy,' said Potts reflectively. 'Smart girl. Ye say she's up there now — when will she be finished?'

'How should I know?' returned Sally, petulantly. 'I don't take the same interest in her doings as ye seem to — and ye a married man, I'll lay odds! Ought to be ashamed o' yourself, ye did indeed!'

Potts moved swiftly to her side and passed an arm about her waist.

'Jealous, my pretty?'

She raised the wet scrubbing brush threateningly, and he fled in alarm.

Chapter VIII: Lost and Found

It was late in the afternoon when the two ladies returned from their exploration of Lewes castle. Miss Ellis admitted that for once she was tired.

'I dare say we shall be glad of an early night, my love,' she said, sinking into a chair in Elizabeth's bedchamber. 'After all, we have almost three hours travelling before us tomorrow, and we had no proper rest last night.'

Elizabeth agreed, but it was evident that her mind was elsewhere. After a moment, Miss Ellis asked her what was the matter.

Elizabeth shrugged. 'Oh, nothing! Or at least — yes, there is something, Margaret! What do you suppose he can mean by it?'

Her friend did not pretend to misunderstand. 'I really have no notion at all, my dear. Perhaps — as you remarked this morning — it could simply be coincidence. How else can one pass the time but by strolling about the town?'

'Yes, but to stroll in exactly the same direction as ourselves on two separate occasions! That is surely more than coincidence.'

'Well,' replied Miss Ellis, with a twinkle in her eye, 'it is either accident or design, as you choose. Which would you prefer it to be?'

'Pray, don't be nonsensical, Margaret! Why should he follow me about when he will not even give any sign that he has recognised me? It does not make sense at all!'

'Unless he is trying to recall who you are, as I suggested this morning. He may realise that he has previously met you somewhere, without being able to fix on the time and place or your name. In such a case, he might very well try to keep you in sight until recollection returns.'

'That is not a very flattering notion,' said Elizabeth, with a sigh.

Miss Ellis glanced sharply at her, started to speak, then changed her mind. She watched in silence while Elizabeth moved restlessly about the room for a few moments, dangling her bonnet from one finger by its ribbon.

'My dear,' she ventured to say at last, 'I fear that this unexpected encounter with Mr. Farnham may have brought back to you some of the painful feelings which —'

Elizabeth halted before the dressing-table, staring down at it absentmindedly. 'No. No, you are quite wrong, Margaret,' she answered, quietly.

'If you say so, my love.'

'I do say so,' Elizabeth said, in a stronger voice. 'Don't imagine that I have been nourishing a hopeless passion for — for Mr. Farnham during all these past six years. There was a time, it is true — However, I need not tell you that the emotions of a girl of nineteen are not likely to survive unchanged for such a long period without any encouragement. A year or two, perhaps, at the most — I have long since put the whole affair out of my mind. Let us talk of something else.' Her eyes came into focus on the contents of the dressing-table. 'Where is the guide book? Have you moved it? I thought I might read those pages on Lewes castle which we hadn't time to look at this morning.'

Miss Ellis recognised that *A Tour of Sussex* was to be used to steer the conversation away from the previous subject, and did her best to concur in this scheme by rising from her chair to assist in looking for the book. The search began half-heartedly, neither quite believing in it; but before long both were looking in earnest, every other thought for the moment put aside.

'Well, it isn't here,' declared Elizabeth, after they had searched in vain throughout both the rooms, neglecting no possible hiding place. 'That's very odd! Now where could it have gone?'

'Perhaps one of the maids removed it by mistake when they were doing our rooms,' suggested Miss Ellis.

'Or perhaps someone else managed to sneak in and take it away while the rooms were unlocked and the maids were busy elsewhere,' said Elizabeth, slowly.

'Oh, but that's absurd! Why should anyone do so? It is not a valuable book, you know. Anyone may buy a copy in almost any bookshop for a few shillings.'

'But not this copy, Margaret. This copy, you may recall, had a letter in the back — a letter addressed to a Mr. J. Martin, of Crowle Manor.'

Margaret frowned. 'You think that has something to do with the disappearance of the book? No, that won't answer, Elizabeth. If anyone knew the letter was there in the first place, a moment's search in the book would have shown that it was there no longer.'

'Yes, I know. But —' Elizabeth paused, thinking rapidly. 'Perhaps whoever took the book didn't have time to examine it on the spot. I dare say it had to be done very quickly — this person may have slipped in while the maids were cleaning the rooms, and dared not linger for fear of being noticed, but smuggled the book out to examine it elsewhere at leisure. And then, of course, whoever it was would discover later that the letter was no longer there.'

'But then, my dear,' said Miss Ellis, in a tone of one talking to a somewhat backward child, 'the only person who could know that the letter was in the book would be the person who put it there originally; and it is inconceivable that the same person would want to remove it now. Unless, of course, we really are dealing with a maniac — which I sometimes think we must be. Either that, or we are run mad ourselves!'

'I don't know,' replied Elizabeth, doubtfully. 'I just don't know. But one thing seems clear, at all events — there is something very odd about that packet for J. Martin, Esquire.'

'I suppose you still have it safe?' asked Margaret sharply.

They went at once to look, and both heaved a sigh of relief when they found the packet still in Elizabeth's letter case, where she had put it.

'To my mind, this whole affair is nothing but a storm in a tea cup!' exclaimed Miss Ellis. 'I dare say the maids removed the book along with some dirty towels, or something! We should certainly question them, and I am sure it will be recovered instantly.'

She was wrong. When they succeeded in tracking down the maid who had cleaned their rooms earlier, the girl certainly recalled the book, as she had lifted it in order to dust the dressing-table; but she was positive that it had been replaced there when she had finished, and that no one could have moved it since, as she had locked the doors of both rooms on completing them. She was evidently anxious lest the ladies should think she had purloined it, and made haste to inform them that she could not even read. Her face paled when Miss Ellis spoke of reporting the matter to the landlady.

'Please, ma'am,' she pleaded, 'if only ye'll give me a little time, I'll comb the whole place till I find it, 'deed I will! For it must be somewheres, ma'am — and who would want a thing like that, beggin' y'r pardon, I'm sure, ma'am — it must have got took by mistake, though I'm ready to swear as it was 'ere when I locked the room, an' how it could vanish, unless someone come in by the key'ole, is more'n I can think! But if only ye won't tell Missus, not yet awhile — for I swears I never took it, but Missus'll like as not turn me off without a character if even she gets to 'ear of it — an' what'll become of me then I don't know... 'Deed, ma'am — ladies both,' she finished, bursting into tears, 'I never took y'r book — honest, I never—'

'There, there, don't cry,' said Elizabeth, patting the girl's arm consolingly. 'We don't believe for one moment that you stole the book, so we shall not report its loss to Mrs. Jilkes, if you will be blamed. But do your best to find it for us, there's a good girl. It is of sentimental value.'

The girl promised eagerly that she would, and went away comforted.

'I'm sure it happened as I suspected,' said Elizabeth. 'Someone managed to get in here for a moment while the maids had turned their backs, snatched the book up and took it away to a safe place before examining it.'

'Which brings us back to the point where we started,' said Miss Ellis dryly.

'Why should anyone do so? Well, yes, that is the puzzle.' Elizabeth took a turn or two about the room, then swung round suddenly, her blue eyes alert. 'Let's start at the beginning, Margaret. Someone has given us a letter to deliver to Crowle Manor. Now, who knows we are going there?'

Miss Ellis nodded approval of this logical approach to the problem. 'Well, the landlord for one, of course. You asked him for a chaise to Crowle. Also,' she added, as an afterthought, 'Mr. Farnham, who was standing close enough at hand to overhear your request — and, yes, that insufferable female who travelled down with us — what is her name? Mrs. Wood, that's it.'

'Mrs. Wood!' exclaimed Elizabeth, excitedly. 'Yes, of course, Mrs. Wood! Now there we might have hit upon something, Margaret! I never mentioned the house to the landlord, you know — I simply asked for a conveyance to Crowle. But Mrs. Wood heard me mention Crowle *Manor* in the Mail coach — I told you how she pricked up her ears at it. Now, I wonder...'

She relapsed into thought for a few moments, while Miss Ellis watched her in silence.

'I think I have it,' she said, at last, triumphantly. 'Margaret, do you suppose that the packet could possibly contain any kind of contraband?'

'Contraband? My dear Elizabeth —'

'It is not so ridiculous as it sounds,' continued Elizabeth, anticipating her friend's criticism. 'Only cast your mind back to our journey, Margaret, for a moment. Do you recall the coach stopping for those men to make a search of the mail box?'

Margaret nodded. 'Perfectly.'

'Well, perhaps you also recall that Mrs. Wood was very upset about the delay, so that she became almost rude to us?'

'Completely rude, I should have said, myself.'

'Just so. Well, at the time I could not quite see why she was so upset; but I did have a hazy kind of notion that she was afraid of something or other. Now I begin to see what it might have been. You may remember that I could not quite hear what the men were saying, but I repeated the little I did hear, and that was something about a search. Mrs. Wood immediately asked if I meant they were going to search the coach. Now I think of it, she was decidedly alarmed at the notion.'

'I imagine anyone might well be,' replied Miss Ellis, reasonably. 'It is not a pleasant thing to have one's baggage searched, I am sure, although thank goodness it has never happened to me.'

'But there was more in her manner than a natural shrinking from such an intrusion on her privacy,' insisted Elizabeth. 'Margaret, I am convinced that she was afraid of what a search might reveal — and I am not thinking of the more intimate items of a female's personal attire, either! It's my belief that she was carrying some kind of contraband — and if I am right, and it is contained in that packet —'

'Fustian, my dear! What kind of contraband could be contained there? Only tea — and scarcely enough of that to be worth anyone's while in smuggling!'

'I don't know what it is,' persisted Elizabeth, disregarding this scathing interruption, 'but I know how Mrs. Wood could have put the packet in the guide book — or rather, I can guess. There was a moment when we had our backs turned to her so that we could not have seen what she was doing. And if you remember, Margaret —' Elizabeth paused impressively — 'the guide book had fallen on to the floor when the coach stopped so violently. It would be quite close at her hand. She had only to remove the packet from wherever she had it concealed, slip it into the empty pocket at the back of the book, and push the book under the seat, hoping it might be overlooked if a search did take place —'

'Well, of course,' admitted Miss Ellis, grudgingly, 'it could have happened as you say. But it all seems so improbable, to say the least —'

'And then,' went on Elizabeth, 'when we alighted at Lewes, taking the guide book with us, there was only one thing for her to do. That was to try and recover her packet, if possible before we should happen to find it. So —' she paused a moment, then continued in a flash of triumph — 'so she came into my room while I was resting early this morning, but I woke up before she could recover her property. That meant she had to try again later. We made it more difficult by locking our rooms — do you remember, she walked by us just as we were doing so? She must have realised then that her only chance would be to slip in when the maids were doing the cleaning. And that's exactly what she did — but by then, of course, we'd already removed the packet from the back of the book. There, what do you think of that?'

'Masterly, my dear. But you are not now constructing a plot for one of your novels, you know. If that packet contains anything but letters, or some other kind of papers, then I am someone other than Margaret Ellis!'

Elizabeth frowned. 'Yes,' she said slowly. 'It certainly did not feel like anything else when I handled it. And yet this is an explanation which fits so many of the facts —'

'I don't entirely agree,' demurred Miss Ellis. 'What about the pedlar and his mention of a letter to Crowle? You haven't suggested anything to fit that fact, so far. You think now that he has nothing to do with the business, after all?'

'I don't know,' began Elizabeth. 'There may be some connection —'

She was interrupted by a knock on the door. Miss Ellis opened it, and saw their chambermaid standing outside.

'If ye please, ma'am,' she said, smiling broadly, 'I've found your book.'

She handed *A Tour of Sussex* to Miss Ellis, who took it and turned to Elizabeth with an amused smile.

'There you are, you see! Where did you find it?' she asked, turning back to the abigail.

'If ye please, ma'am, in the chambermaids' cupboard where we keeps all the cleaning things. It must have got took there by mistake. I'm that sorry, ma'am, I'm sure.'

Miss Ellis thanked the girl and dismissed her, closing the door.

'Well, my dear,' she remarked, her smile widening. 'You see it was all a fantasy. The book was taken by the maids in error, just as I supposed.'

'And the letter?' asked Elizabeth challengingly.

Chapter IX: Night of Terror

Tired though she was, Elizabeth found it difficult to sleep that night. For one thing, the weather was oppressive, and her room seemed hot and airless, in spite of the slightly opened window. She tossed and turned in her bed, thinking over the events of the past twenty-four hours.

Strange, to have met Robert Farnham, after six years without either sight or sound of him. She thought of their lightning love affair, and smiled wistfully to herself in the darkness. She had been so young, so ready to fall in love with the first attractive young man who had paid her any attentions; and he, in his quick decisive way, had seemed to single her out at once. She had never known very much about his background. At the time, they were both visiting in the neighbourhood of Tonbridge Wells, and frequently found themselves in social gatherings at the same households. Her aunt had seemed satisfied that he was a young man of good connections and easy means, although she was not personally acquainted with his family. She had smiled on the growing friendship between Mr. Farnham and her niece, confident that Elizabeth's brother and guardian, Edward, would pursue any necessary inquiries into the young man's affairs.

But there had been no formal application to Edward Thorne: Elizabeth herself had sent her lover packing.

She could not bring herself to desert Anne. Her maternal feeling for her younger sister had sprung up at the moment their nurse had placed the new-born babe in the three-year-old Elizabeth's arms. The sudden loss of both their parents, the necessity of sharing a new home with an unsympathetic sister-in-law, only deepened the feeling of responsibility towards Anne which had always been there in some measure. Recently, she had slowly come to accept the fact that her sister, now happily married, needed her care no longer, and that she herself was free to live her own life; but at the time of Robert Farnham's courtship, Anne's interests had come first.

It had been useless for Farnham to protest that Anne could share their home when they were married, that everything between the two sisters could remain unchanged. Elizabeth realised that such an arrangement could not be a happy one for any of them. Anne had been too used to claiming a monopoly of her elder sister's thoughts and interests; she would never take kindly to second place.

Torn between conflicting loyalties, Elizabeth had asked him to wait; but waiting was not in Robert Farnham's line.

'If you are uncertain now,' he had said, bitterly, 'you will be even less certain next year, and the year after that. No, you must take me now — or never.'

Perhaps, thought Elizabeth, he had hoped to force her hand by that ultimatum. If so, he had misjudged her character. They parted, both hiding deeper hurts than they cared to let the other see; and in a few days he had left the neighbourhood and Elizabeth had returned to her brother's house. Since then, she had always found an excuse to avoid paying her Aunt Mary a visit, and for some time afterwards had dreaded a letter from Tunbridge Wells for fear it might contain some reference to the young man whom her aunt believed had not 'come up to scratch, after all.' Her fears proved groundless, however, for Aunt Mary understood girls too well to remind them of lost lovers.

Did he still remember anything of the past, Elizabeth wondered? And had he recognised her, or not? Surely if he had, he must have made some acknowledgement — a slight bow, a formal 'Good day'? It was the least civility he could offer. Perhaps she had changed so greatly that he really did not know her again. Margaret said she had not, but Margaret was too partial to be relied upon. Six years was a long time, and no doubt some of her early bloom had gone. At one time, she knew, she had been considered attractive; but it was some years now since anyone had told her so. There had been no suitors to follow Robert Farnham. Elizabeth realised that this had been partly her own fault, for she had failed to respond to any of the few eligible young men whom she had chanced to meet since, and they had soon turned their thoughts in more rewarding directions. It seemed she was destined to become an old maid. She told herself that it was not because she cherished an undying love for Robert Farnham. She had ceased to think of him many years ago. It was more that love seemed to her to be an experience that was over and done with; rather like the measles, she reflected ruefully, which one would not expect to get more than once.

The room suddenly seemed unbearably oppressive. She flung back the coverlet and slid from the bed. Groping her way to the window, she moved aside the curtains and quietly raised the lower sash, thrusting her head out so that she might take in grateful breaths of the cool night air. A cloud-harried moon sailed across the sky, its fitful light falling on the stable clock, which showed the hands creeping towards two. The yard was deserted, the horses quiet in their stalls, the whole inn slept. It seemed that she was the only being awake in the whole universe.

Not quite: even as the thought entered her mind, a shadowy figure began to cross the yard from the stables. She watched idly for a moment, then quickly drew in her head as she saw that the figure was moving in the direction of her window. She drew the curtains partly across, and stood behind their masking folds, peering out.

It was not that she expected anything of interest to happen. For all she knew, someone might cross the inn yard at this hour every night, bound on some routine errand. But here was a living creature to share her vigil in an otherwise sleeping world; she felt an urge to retain the tenuous human contact.

The figure came to a halt almost underneath her window. The moon escaped momentarily from a cloak of cloud, its light falling upon a face which Elizabeth knew at once — the crafty face of the pedlar. He looked about him as the stable clock rustily struck two.

A moment later, a second figure glided from the shadows to join him. A cloud began to move across the moon, but not before Elizabeth had time to recognise this new arrival. It was their late travelling companion, Mrs. Wood.

A startled exclamation escaped her, and she quickly clapped her hand over her mouth, afraid that the sound might have betrayed her presence. She soon realised that she need not have worried. The couple began to converse, and although she could just manage to detect the low murmur of their voices, it was impossible to hear anything they were saying.

It never once crossed her mind that she ought not to eavesdrop on their conversation. She had been involved in so many strange events since she left London, that this even stranger nocturnal meeting seemed to be very much her concern. Why were two such unlikely people meeting by stealth at this hour of the night? The answer must have some bearing on those other mysterious incidents. If she could only hear what they were saying, everything might be made clear to her.

The clouds were still shielding the moon, so she ventured to thrust her head out of the window in an effort to hear better. To her disappointment, this made no difference at all, and she soon drew back, fearful of being seen. She remained behind the shelter of the curtains, watching the couple in the stableyard with a growing sense of frustration.

At last, she came to a desperate decision: she would go downstairs, let herself out of the side door of the inn and try to creep near enough to Potts and Mrs. Wood to overhear their conversation.

If she had paused to consider, she would most likely have lost the courage to embark on such a venture, but she did not allow herself time to think. She snatched a pelisse from the closet; buttoned it over her nightgown, and thrust her bare feet into the soft kid sandals she had been wearing earlier.

She hesitated before lighting her bedside candle. A light might be dangerous, for it would advertise her presence; but without it, she could not trust herself to find her way around without stumbling into some article of furniture at the risk of waking the household. She lit the candle, and, softly opening the door, crept out into the passage.

She glided swiftly down the stairs, turning at the foot along the passage which she knew led to the rear quarters of the inn. It did not take her long to reach the side door.

She was not surprised to find that it was neither locked nor bolted: Mrs. Wood must have come out this way. No doubt she had used the service staircase which began quite close to her room, Number Seven, and ended only a few yards from the side door. It would be a quicker route for her than the main staircase, and there would be less danger of disturbing the other residents, as it did not take her past any of their rooms.

Elizabeth set her candle down on the floor so that she could use both hands, then quietly lifted the latch and eased the door open.

The candle flickered in the sudden draught. She turned to shield it, but she was too late. The flame died, leaving a smell of hot tallow. The door, released from her restraining hand, swung back with a creak that seemed deafening in the nocturnal silence. Alarmed, she snatched up the candlestick and stood still, listening.

She heard footsteps approaching from outside.

In a sudden panic, she looked about her for somewhere to hide; but no friendly moon sent a beam of light through the open door to relieve the gloom of the passage, and her eyes had not yet adjusted to the loss of the candle.

As the footsteps drew nearer to the open door, she pressed hard back against the wall of the passage, her heart pounding. A door swung inwards behind her so suddenly that she almost fell into the room beyond. Recovering herself quickly, she groped for the handle on the inside and pushed the door as nearly shut as she dared, fearing to close it completely lest the click of the latch should betray her presence. Still clutching her useless candlestick, she cowered against the wall immediately behind the door. It was the best she could do to conceal herself, and might serve if only the pedlar and Mrs. Wood did not actually enter the room.

Her straining ears heard the footsteps pause on the threshold of the outer door. A low murmur of voices followed, and the footsteps came into the passage, halting outside the room where she crouched, hiding. A beam of light crept through the crack in the door, but Elizabeth was too painfully intent on what was happening outside in the passage to gain any advantage from the slight illumination by taking stock of her surroundings.

The lowered voice of Mrs. Wood came to her clearly. 'I tell you I left it fastened. Someone has been through since.'

'Well, there's no one here, is there?' It was the pedlar's voice, insolent in tone. 'And no one could've been out in the yard without me noticing, don't ye fret.'

'What about these rooms leading off the passage?' asked Mrs. Wood sharply. 'Someone might be hiding in one of them.'

The words made Elizabeth's blood freeze.

'That's soon settled,' replied Potts. 'We'll take a look, shall we? There's only two on 'em this end. Unless ye'd like me to search in all the kitchen quarters?'

'Mind your tongue, unless you wish to be reported to your betters! No, I think the two nearest rooms are the most likely.'

'And I don't reckon anyone else has been through that door at all,' stated Potts, bluntly. 'But since ye'll have it so —'

Almost paralysed by fear, Elizabeth waited for her door to be flung open.

But evidently the pair had decided to investigate first the room on the opposite side of the passage, for the light and the low voices moved away. Now that the danger was postponed for a while, Elizabeth's numbed brain began to work at lightning speed. Would it be any use her making a dash for safety while they were searching the room opposite? In daylight, she might have risked it; but without a light, and not knowing her way about the inn very well, it seemed certain that she would betray her presence. In the end, she remained where she was. This was just as well, for in a very short time, she heard the couple return and once more the crack of light appeared.

Before she could recover from the sudden panic which overcame her, the door of her hideaway was thrust open until it came to rest only an inch or two from her body. Potts advanced a little way over the threshold, and holding a dark lantern high in one hand, looked keenly round the room.

Fortunately, it was so sparsely furnished that it was at once obvious to him that there could be no cover there for even a cat. It appeared to be some kind of storage closet, with shelves against the walls and a wooden table in the centre. Cowering behind the open door, Elizabeth feverishly willed the pedlar not to advance any farther into the room. If he should move so that he could see behind the door, she was completely undone.

After what seemed an age, he drew back into the passage, pulling the door to behind him, without fully closing it.

'No one there,' she heard him say, in a low tone. 'Reckon ye must have left the side door unlatched when ye came through into the yard. Careless, that's what.'

'How dare you take that insolent tone with me!' hissed Mrs. Wood. 'I did no such thing — I'm not quite a fool.'

'Not done too well, though, so far, have ye?' Elizabeth, still cowering in terror, could hear the low, mocking tones quite plainly. 'There's them as won't be too pleased to hear as ye've lost what they sent me to get, and so I warn ye.'

'It is not lost, because I know perfectly well where it is, and mean to recover it without delay,' answered the woman, acidly. 'I will find a way of letting you know when I've done so. Meanwhile, I'm going to my room, and I advise you to go, too. I don't like the look of things. We can't find anyone here, but all the same, someone did open that door. I'll bolt it behind you. Go now, and you'll hear from me later.'

Potts mumbled something which Elizabeth could not quite catch. Then she heard his footsteps retreating, followed by the subdued click of a latch, and the quiet sound of a door-bolt being eased gently into place.

After that, there followed a few moments of pregnant silence. Elizabeth had her hand to her mouth, pressing her teeth into it so viciously that the marks could still be seen on the following day. It was the only way in which she could stop herself from letting out some unguarded exclamation of fright. Only the door of the room divided her from the woman who still lingered suspiciously outside, unconvinced by the pedlar's assurance that there was no one in the vicinity. She might push open the door any minute, thought Elizabeth in near panic; she might come right into the room, instead of standing on the threshold as the pedlar had done. If she did, then she would be bound to see its terrified occupant crouching behind the door. And then — but fright had sealed up the flow of Elizabeth's imagination, and for once her mind could not move beyond the present hazard.

It could have been only a few moments that Mrs. Wood stood hesitating in the passage, but to Elizabeth it seemed like hours. At length, her straining ears detected soft footfalls retreating along the passage, and the pale gleam of light which had shown through the crack in the door vanished, leaving the darkness complete.

There could be no doubt that at last Mrs. Wood had gone.

It was some time before Elizabeth could persuade her reason to accept this fact, and longer still before she had sufficient control over her limbs to attempt to move. But after a while she gained some mastery over her emotions; she straightened up and moved forward, still clutching her candlestick, groping with her other hand for the edge of the door.

She had just started to pull it open, when she again heard the sound of stealthy footsteps coming along the passage towards the side door of the inn.

She drew back in renewed alarm. Was it Mrs. Wood returning? She listened with straining ears and presently realised that the footsteps, although muffled, had a more solid sound than the thin patter of a woman's light sandals. Was it the pedlar? But that was impossible, for she had heard him go out into the yard, and Mrs. Wood had bolted the door after him. Then who could it be?

The answer, no doubt, was that someone — most likely the landlord — had heard a noise and had come downstairs to investigate. If so, she was in imminent danger of discovery. And how on earth would she be able to explain why she was cowering here in the darkness?

One thing was clear; she must not let herself be seen. If it should be the landlord, though, he would most likely look into every room on the ground floor; and he was heading this way.

The footsteps drew nearer, until they halted outside the room where she was hiding.

She drew back behind the shelter of the door, striving with all her might to flatten herself against the wall so that if the door should be pushed open once more she would escape observation as she had done before.

She tried not to heed the warning inner voice which told her she would be very lucky to succeed a second time. She waited, hardly daring to breathe, expecting that at any moment the door would swing back, and she would be discovered at last.

The seconds lengthened into minutes, each one of them seeming like an hour, and still the dreaded moment did not come. And then she realised that faint but unmistakeable sounds were coming to her ears which suggested that far from taking an interest in the door of her hideaway, the new arrival on the scene was engaged in stealthily opening the side door of the inn. She heard his footsteps softly crossing the threshold; in a few moments they were lost to her altogether. Evidently he had gone out into the yard, she thought, and in the first flood of relief she almost forgot that the danger was not yet over. But even as she groped for the door handle to make her escape, a thought came which froze her to the spot.

Whoever had gone out into the yard might return at any moment. If she were to go blundering into the passage now she might run into him.

Every instinct urged flight upon her, but she forced herself to listen to the voice of reason. Once outside this door, she would have a fairly long stretch of corridor to cover before she came to the bend which led to the staircase. Without a light, it would take her some time to grope her way along; and anyone entering by the side door must see her at once, provided he was carrying a light himself, which was almost certain.

There was nothing else for it but to cower in her corner in the dark little room until she heard those footsteps returning. Then all she could hope for was that the owner of them would be satisfied without a further search, and would return to bed. After allowing a reasonable interval to elapse, she could do the same herself. At that moment, to be safe and sound in her bed seemed to Elizabeth to represent the pinnacle of human happiness and achievement.

The second thoughts prevailed, and she remained where she was. Afterwards, she calculated that it could not have been more than half an hour, although at the time it seemed a great deal longer. The worst of her panic had subsided, but she still felt a little weak at the knees. Once she found herself repenting of her decision, and, greatly daring, she peered round the door into the passage. Perhaps if she made a quick dash — even as she poised herself ready, she heard the faint sound of the side door opening. She drew back quickly, her heart starting to pound again. The man had returned. Once again, fear took possession of her.

This time, her ordeal was not protracted. She heard the door quietly closed and bolted, and afterwards stealthy footsteps moved past her room and along the passage until they faded into the distance. Whoever it was had gone, this time presumably for good.

Even though she felt tolerably certain of this she forced herself to wait five or ten minutes longer. The continued silence had subdued her panic, and she felt almost easy again as she crept round the door and felt her way cautiously along the dark passage and up the stairs to her room. As she had supposed, her progress was slow without the aid of a light, and she could only feel thankful that she had not attempted to return while there had been any likelihood of discovery. Even now, she reminded herself, an incautious step might cause her to blunder into some obstacle and raise the rest of the house.

At last, she stood outside the door of her bedchamber. Grasping the knob firmly, she let herself quietly into the room and closed the door thankfully behind her.

She moved towards the bedside table, and, groping for the tinder box, lit her candle once more, setting it down with a great sigh of relief...

As she turned round again a figure moved out of the shadow towards her.

Before she could cry out, an arm like a vice encircled her, and a hand was clapped firmly over her mouth.

Chapter X: At Cross Purposes

'Don't scream!' The command was spoken in a low tone, but it carried conviction. 'If you do, I must take measures we would both have cause to regret.'

She had begun to struggle, but froze into immobility on hearing the voice of her captor. She turned a frightened, incredulous gaze on Robert Farnham.

'You can't escape me, so don't try,' he warned her grimly, keeping his hand over her mouth. 'I must talk to you. Promise not to cry out, and I'll release you at once. You only have to nod your head.'

She continued to stare at him for a moment or two; then she attempted a nod.

He released her and stood back a little, looking at her in silence. Her face was pale and strained; her brown hair tumbled about her shoulders, and from time to time she gave a little shiver. She looked like a frightened child, but no compassion showed in the man's eyes as they rested on her.

'So it was you, after all.' His voice was harsh. 'I suspected it all along, but I did not want to think it true.'

'What are you doing here?' Between shock and fright, Elizabeth could scarcely force her trembling lips to frame the words. 'You have no right — leave this room instantly!'

He laughed in an unpleasant way. 'The innocent maiden, eh? Doing it too brown, my girl! It's not the first time there's been a man in your room by all accounts, and I dare swear it won't be the last. B'God, you've changed since first we met — but there's no profit in thinking of that —'

'So you *did* recognise me?' stammered Elizabeth, in her confused state of mind seizing upon the one thing in his speech that made any sense to her.

He pursed his lips. 'Not at first. You were changed — there was something different about your hair, for one thing. But after I'd passed close to you I knew you, right enough.'

Elizabeth sank into a chair with a weary gesture. 'Hair styles do change in six years,' she said mechanically. 'But this is neither the time nor the place for a discussion of that kind. I am very tired. Please leave me now.'

'You were not too tired to creep down into the stable yard and keep an assignation with the pedlar,' he retorted, grimly. 'And I've no intention of leaving here until I get what I came for, so make your mind up to that.'

'An assignation with the pedlar — I?' asked Elizabeth, whipped out of her exhaustion by a sudden gust of anger. 'Upon my word, you must have run mad, sir!'

'I wish I were indeed mad,' he replied, sombrely, 'and then I could think all this a mere hallucination. But you'll not trick me with your airs of injured innocence, madam — I know you for what you are.'

'Indeed! And what is that, may I ask?'

'There are no words bad enough to describe it,' he replied, harshly. 'To think what you once were — and what you have become!'

She flung back her head and her blue eyes glinted coldly in the candlelight.

'You shall no longer stay here and insult me. Leave this room at once, or I scream for help!'

'B'God, you'll not!'

In two strides he was bending over her, one hand behind her head and the other covering her mouth.

'I don't leave this room until you've given me the papers,' he muttered, glaring into her defiant eyes. 'If it's necessary to bind and gag you in order to get them, I shall do so, never doubt. So don't rely on my chivalry, my dear — I know all the tricks practiced by those of your dirty trade.'

Elizabeth stared at him aghast. There was nothing else for it, she thought agitatedly, he must be out of his mind. What ought she to do? One scream from her must succeed in rousing Margaret, who although she was a fairly sound sleeper, could not fail to hear a noise of such an alarming kind through the thin partition wall which divided the two rooms. But if Margaret were to be aroused, so might others, and Elizabeth's mind shrank from the public scene which must ensue. In her view, dramatic scenes were best confined to their proper medium, the stage; she preferred to avoid them whenever possible in everyday life.

Something of what she was thinking must have shown in her expression, or possibly the man who held her in such an ungentle grip must have known her well enough to guess at her thoughts.

After a moment, he said: 'You won't wish to bring the whole house about your ears, I know. Promise not to scream, and I'll release you.'

She nodded, and at once he stood back from her.

She massaged her cheek where his fingers had dug into it, but for the moment she could not summon up enough energy to speak.

'You've only yourself to blame,' he said, a trifle on the defensive as he watched her. 'If you choose to tangle in rough work, you can't expect to be handled with kid gloves.'

'I should be less at a disadvantage,' she said icily, 'if I had the remotest notion what you were talking about.'

He made an impatient gesture. 'Oh, for pity's sake, you don't think to take me in with such fustian?'

'It happens to be the truth.'

'Very likely,' he said, contemptuously. 'No doubt we have totally different notions of the truth, you and I. No, it's no use trying to play the innocent, my girl — I saw you from my window, there in the yard with Potts the pedlar, so the game's up.'

'You saw someone else — not me.'

'Oh? Then exactly where have *you* been? After I'd spotted the couple through the window, I came along to your room and looked in, suspecting that the female might be you. Sure enough you were missing, and you've only just returned. Talk your way out of that, if you can.'

'I am not accountable to you for my actions,' replied Elizabeth, coldly. 'I think, in the circumstances, I'm justified in asking why you should ever have entertained the suspicion that the female with the pedlar was myself.'

'You want to know how I rumbled you, eh? Very well, I've no objection to telling you — it might prove a salutary lesson. The first thing was when I overheard you asking the landlord for a conveyance to take you to Crowle. That place name was one of the few clues I had to this affair. You see, the letter you left in the grate of the house at Lincoln's Inn Fields was not quite burnt through — it was still possible to make out most of it.' He shook his head mockingly. 'Careless, my dear, very careless. To leave no traces behind you is one of the most elementary rules in the game.'

Elizabeth looked at him with a bewildered air. 'I haven't the remotest notion what you're talking about! What letter? I left no letter in a grate — and I have never been in any house at Lincoln's Inn Fields in my life!'

'God, what a hypocrite!' he exclaimed, in a voice of loathing. 'And this is the girl I once thought I would like to make my wife! I see now what a lucky escape I had, although I thought differently at the time.'

'Yes, and so do I!' retorted Elizabeth, with spirit. 'To think I might have been wed to a raving lunatic!'

For a second a hint of doubt crept into his expression. Then it changed into one of grudging admiration. 'You're a damned good actress madam, among your other dangerous qualities, I'll grant you that! But it's no good — you're beaten. I was there this morning outside the inn when you and your companion were looking at the pedlar's wares, and I heard every word that passed. He offered to deliver a letter for you, and mentioned Crowle. Not only your reply to him but your expression, showed that you knew what he meant, right enough. The assignation for tonight must have been made later, for I'm ready to swear that no sign was given at the time, and I watched you closely enough. I followed you round the town on that damned shopping expedition, too, in case you should hand on the documents to anyone else.'

Elizabeth gave a weak laugh. 'So that was why! And Margaret thought —' She broke off; even in the present circumstances a little colour crept into her pale cheeks at the recollection of what Margaret had thought, and how ready she herself had been to credit it.

The man staring down at her caught for a moment a glimpse of the girl he had known six years ago. His expression softened, and he took a step towards her, one hand stretched out in appeal.

'Elizabeth! I don't know how you came to be embroiled in this sordid business, but I beg you to get out of it at once. I'll make a bargain with you, for old times' sake. Give me the documents, and I'll return them without implicating you — your part in the affair need not be mentioned. But you must go away from here immediately, the farther the better, so that neither side can trace you. If you are short of money —'

But here she interrupted him, starting to her feet.

'You *are* mad! Nothing you say makes sense!'

His expression hardened. 'Very well, if that's the way you want to play the hand. But you must take the consequences. And now you can hand over those documents, for I don't leave without them. No use playing off any more tricks — my patience is running out.'

'What documents?' asked Elizabeth.

She was only playing for time, for she knew very well that he must be referring to the packet which had so strangely appeared in the guide book. She was unable to make head or tail of most of what he had said, but this one point was clear enough. Robert Farnham was one of those who seemed determined to gain possession of the letter addressed to J. Martin, Esquire. But it was by no means clear to Elizabeth whether she ought to allow him to have it. What she had just overheard between Mrs. Wood and Potts the pedlar seemed to confirm her feeling that Mrs. Wood had originally placed the letter in *A Tour of Sussex*, and then afterwards tried to regain possession of it in order, as it now appeared, to pass it on to the pedlar. The motives prompting such a tortuous course of action were too difficult for Elizabeth to fathom in her present exhausted state; but she felt instinctively that they would be discreditable. On the other hand, all that she remembered of Robert Farnham urged her to think well of him. Could the packet be some kind of contraband, and had he any connection with the Customs authorities? But surely the whole affair must be more complex than that, for he was evidently confusing her with some other female; one who by his account was a lady of easy virtue, and who had left lying about somewhere a half-burnt letter which apparently held great significance for him.

His face hardened. 'Very well, if you will have it so, I must find them myself. I know you haven't yet handed them over to the pedlar, for I waylaid him after he left you, and gave both him and his pack a thorough turning over. I am not without experience in these matters, so I know I missed nothing.' He broke off, a puzzled frown wrinkling his brow. 'It beats me, I must confess, why you didn't hand them over there and then in the stable yard — why else did you bother to meet him there?'

'I keep telling you I didn't.' Elizabeth was now rapidly recovering from the harrowing experiences of that evening, and her usual common sense was taking charge. 'Oh, do listen to me for a moment —' as he made an impatient gesture — 'and perhaps we can both learn something, for we seem to be talking at cross purposes. You spoke just now of our earlier friendship, and said that you found it scarcely credible that I should have changed so greatly since last we met. Well, I haven't changed; at least not in essentials.' He shrugged contemptuously, and made as if to speak, but she brushed the effort aside. 'No, wait, I beg you to hear me out without interruption. I think you owe me that much at least.'

He subsided, standing quietly before her, his eyes fixed on her face in an unwinking stare.

'It's evident that you are confusing me with someone else. You speak of my leaving a letter behind somewhere or other, and of my being involved in some dishonourable business — these things are a complete mystery to me. The only thing that makes any kind of sense is your mention of Crowle. I am indeed going to Crowle. I was recently bequeathed Crowle Manor, and intend to live there during the summer months.' She paused, and a puzzled frown settled on her brow. 'Since I arrived at the White Hart, I have come to wonder what there can be at my uncle's former home to arouse such keen interest in so many of the people I have encountered here. There was the female who travelled with us on the coach, whose name I collect to be Mrs. Wood. She seemed to sit up and take notice when I mentioned Crowle Manor quite casually in conversation with my companion, Miss Ellis. At the time, I thought I must have imagined her interest. I do write stories, you know,' she explained a little shyly.

He nodded. 'I didn't. But pray continue with this particular story, which I must confess I find fascinating. The female, Mrs. Wood seemed interested — who else?'

She, hesitated. 'Well — you, of course. And then there was the pedlar. But you tell me that you heard what passed between us, so there is no point in repeating that.'

'I collect that you are trying to make me believe it's pure coincidence that you should be on your way to Crowle Manor at this particular time?'

'How very quickly you do seize on a notion!' retorted Elizabeth in ironic admiration. 'Only I am *not* trying to make you believe anything, indeed, I can't think why I should put myself to so much trouble. I am merely stating what is a fact.'

'And no doubt you are also quite ready to state as a fact that you have positively no knowledge of a packet which was to be delivered to someone staying here at the White Hart?' asked Farnham, with a contemptuous smile.

She hesitated, and he was quick to press home his advantage.

'Ah, I see you do,' he exclaimed, in satisfaction. 'Don't trouble to deny it. Your face is not yet sufficiently schooled for the part you have to play — you would make a bad card-player, Miss Thorne. Is it still Miss Thorne, I wonder? Or have you succeeded in deluding some other man into lending you the shelter of his name?'

'I am beginning to think,' retorted Elizabeth, with a cool smile, 'that you should be writing stories and not I. You have by far the stronger imagination.'

'Very well, ma'am. But let's not waste any more time. I collect that you have the papers I require, so hand them over.'

'Supposing I were in possession of this packet you seem so anxious to obtain,' said Elizabeth in a calm tone, 'can you give me any good reason why I should hand it over to you?'

'I infer from that remark that you expect payment for delivery,' he replied, contemptuously. 'Well, you'll catch cold at that. Let me remind you that I can take it by force, and afterwards hand you over to the law.'

'The law? Then it is — it must be contraband!' exclaimed Elizabeth, almost to herself. 'And you must be a Customs officer — unlikely as it seems.'

He gave her a withering glance. 'Are you still determined to play act? B'God, I've had enough of this! Hand over that packet immediately, or I take it by force.'

'I don't know what you mean by play acting,' she replied, slowly. 'But it's difficult to know what I ought to do. You see, the letter is directed to someone else — to someone at Crowle Manor. It doesn't seem right to hand it to any other person, but, of course, if you represent the law in some sort —'

He ignored this.

'Where is it?' he demanded, almost fiercely.

She shrank back instinctively before his rough tone, then pulled herself together with an effort, and rose to her feet.

'I have it here,' she said, crossing over to the closet.

He followed close on her heels, and watched with narrowed eyes as she pulled out a valise and rummaged inside it. After a moment, she produced a small leather wallet which she unfastened, revealing a quantity of writing-paper and two quill pens in a holder. There were some pockets on one side of the wallet, and she inserted her hand into one of these.

She turned to the man with a look of distress as she brought her hand out empty.

'It's gone!' she gasped. 'The letter's vanished!'

Chapter XI: Doubt

Robert Farnham was a man who normally knew his own mind, but he left Miss Thorne's room that night in some uncertainty. Either she was a most accomplished actress, or else she had been genuinely surprised when she had failed to find the packet which was important to so many people. He had been able to dismiss the rest of her behaviour, her incredulity and protestations of innocence, as a pitiful charade which was an insult to his intelligence; but the expression on her face when she had vainly searched her letter-case had carried more conviction than all the rest of her performance put together.

He could not remember any hint of a talent for acting or, indeed, duplicity of any kind from his acquaintance with her in the past. But how well had he known her, after all? Two months was scarcely long enough for a young man to understand a female's character; particularly not when he was fool enough, thought Farnham bitterly, to fall head over ears in love with her before a week was out. According to his present information, she was now as corrupt as any woman could well be. Either she had changed drastically in the past six years, or else he had always been mistaken in her.

Nevertheless, there was some puzzling elements in this affair. He knew that those who brought the packet from London had been instructed to hand it over to a courier who would be waiting at the White Hart to carry it on the final stage of its journey. Careful investigation had shown him that this courier must be Potts the bagman; yet Miss Thorne had not handed the packet to Potts, as Farnham had good reason to know. Why had she not done so? Because she was bound for Crowle

Manor herself? And if it had been known by those in authority over her that she was going to Crowle Manor why had she been instructed to hand the packet over to the pedlar to deliver there?

It might be, he reflected, that she was playing a double game. If so, she must be a very experienced agent indeed, and could expect to come to an unpleasant end if she failed to watch her step.

At this grim thought, a sudden wave of doubt swept over him. Could he be mistaken? He had been told to find two females, one young and personable, one in middle years, who would be journeying together from London to the White Hart in Lewes at a certain time. Had he found the wrong pair? No, For Miss Thorne and Miss Ellis had been the only two women to arrive together at the inn at the relevant time. Other female visitors had been accompanied by a male, with the exception of Mrs. Wood. That lady had arrived without escort, nor were any friends or relatives awaiting at the inn. This was an unusual circumstance: he paused to consider it.

Suppose Mrs. Wood should be the female he was after, and not Elizabeth Thorne? It was true that two females had been lodging at the house in Lincoln's Inn Fields and that by the time a search of the house was made, they had both disappeared. It had been assumed that they had left for Lewes in company but there was no direct evidence to prove this. What if they had separated, the younger and more intrepid of the two undertaking the delivery of the packet in Lewes, and the older woman making for some other destination? Although naturally most of his attention had been given to Elizabeth and her friend, he had not altogether overlooked Mrs. Wood, for everyone could bear investigation in a mission of this kind. Some of the woman's actions had seemed noteworthy, in view of all he knew. She had shown an interest in the pedlar; and once Farnham had caught her loitering outside Miss Thorne's room, as though about to enter. She had walked away at once when he had come up the stairs, an action which in itself had seemed to him suspicious; for if she had a legitimate errand to Miss Thorne, she would surely have knocked upon the door. He had borne the incident in mind without attaching too much importance to it, for at that time he had been convinced that Miss Thorne was the woman he had been seeking. Then there was a circumstance for which he had only Elizabeth's word — the fact that Mrs. Wood had shown a marked interest on hearing Miss Thorne and Miss Ellis talking in the Mail coach of their visit to Crowle Manor.

But if Mrs. Wood had brought the packet from London, how did it come to be in Miss Thorne's possession at all? That was a question which he might have done well to put to Elizabeth. He would have done so had he felt any doubts during their recent interview of her complicity in the business. Strange that he should have felt so certain of her guilt while he was with her, and that now doubts should be creeping in. He shrugged: there was no accounting for second thoughts, but it was best not to ignore them. Assuming for the moment that it had been Mrs. Wood who had met Potts in the stable yard and not Miss Thorne, how could Elizabeth's absence from her room at the same time be explained?

He swore softly to himself. It could not, unless she knew more than she was willing to admit. She was concerned in this affair in some way — she must be.

His quick mind followed the notion of Mrs. Wood as the original courier. Under pretence of buying ribbons from the pedlar, she had no doubt made the assignation for tonight. By some means or other, Elizabeth Thorne had tricked her out of the letter, and she had been forced to keep the appointment empty-handed. He nodded: this was borne out by his failure to find the letter when he had searched the pedlar's effects. So now, since Elizabeth no longer had the letter — and he knew she had not, unless it was hidden in her companion's room — it was most likely that Mrs. Wood had succeeded in recovering it. She must have accomplished this during the time that Elizabeth was out of her room, and before he had entered it. Which meant that, while he had been talking to Elizabeth in her room, Mrs. Wood might well have been handing the letter over to Potts.

Having reached this alarming conclusion, he gave up thought in favour of action. Taking up a small dark-lantern which he used on such occasions, he made his way for the second time that night out of the inn and across the yard to the stables.

Inside, he swiftly mounted the ladder leading to the hay loft where Potts slept, and, reaching the trap door, raised it a few cautious inches. All was dark and silent within, except for the faint rustle of a marauding mouse. After listening for a few more minutes, he opened the trap door wide, swinging his body through the aperture with a lithe movement. The hay which was strewn over the floor muffled the sound of his landing. He knew the place from his previous visit, and took cover behind some bales of hay close at hand.

There seemed no sign of life: even the mice were silent, startled by his alien presence. On his previous visit, he had put Potts temporarily to sleep by an effective, but not vicious, blow while he carried out his search. The man should have recovered his senses some time ago, and now would be sleeping naturally, if at all.

Farnham waited a while, straining his ears for any movement, any sound of breathing that might advertise the pedlar's presence. As the minutes ticked by and he heard nothing, the conviction grew on him steadily that Potts was no longer in the loft. At last he stepped out from behind the concealing bales of hay. Adjusting a shutter on the dark-lantern, he directed a beam of light around him.

He saw at once an indentation in some loose hay where a body had recently been lying, and beside it muddy footprints leading towards the trap door. It need only a few more moments to assure him that Potts and his pack had gone.

He left the loft without further delay, going cautiously to the stall where he knew the pedlar's horse was stabled. He had been there earlier, leaving nothing to chance in his search for the letter.

As he feared, the stall was empty now; Potts had ridden off into the night.

The discovery did not dismay Farnham to any extent. If Potts had the packet with him, then he would be taking it to Crowle Manor; if he had not, and his flight had been caused solely by Farnham's recent rough treatment of him, then the packet would still be in the possession of Miss Thorne and her companion. They too, would take it to its appointed destination. Either way, the trail led to Crowle and he must reach there without undue delay.

There was another possibility which did not seem very probable, although he could not afford to overlook it. This was that Mrs. Wood might be in possession of the packet, having taken it from Miss Thorne, but failed to pass it on to Potts. If so, she, too, would try to convey it to Crowle, or else pass it on to someone else who could. So the woman would need watching; but that must be a task for someone else. He must have help. Fortunately, he knew where to go for it, and could find it close at hand.

Soft-footed, he left the stables and headed through the archway of the inn towards the dark, deserted streets of the town.

Chapter XII: At Crowle Manor

'It was easy to see,' concluded Elizabeth, 'that he didn't believe one word of what I'd told him.'

'I suppose one can hardly blame the gentleman,' replied Margaret Ellis. 'It is such a very odd story. I can scarcely credit it myself. But all the same, as he once knew you so intimately —'

'Oh, that is nothing to the purpose,' put in Elizabeth, hurriedly. 'People change with the years — it is a mistake to suppose they do not. No, what I find difficult to understand, Margaret, is what Mr. Farnham's interest in this strange affair can possibly be.'

'He did not enlighten you?'

Elizabeth shook her head. 'He threw out a number of remarks which led me to suppose that he had some connection with the law, or the Customs authorities. But as to saying anything definite, no. Neither could I learn from him exactly what was in the mysterious packet. He insisted on behaving as if I knew very well what it contained, and could lead him to it, if I chose. He even,' she finished, with a blush, 'went so far as to search my baggage himself, when I could not find the letter.'

Miss Ellis exclaimed in horror. 'My dear child, you should have called me to your aid! I would soon have sent him about his business!'

'Yes, Margaret, but it did seem to be very much his business; and even though he would not explain himself, I feel very strongly that I ought not to hinder him. There is something of the utmost importance, I feel sure, behind all the odd incidents which have occurred since we left London.' A worried frown settled on her brow. 'And yet, suppose I have it all wrong? Suppose the pedlar and Mrs. Wood have a right to the packet, and Mr. Farnham is seeking to obtain illicit possession of it? I almost wish it had been left in our charge and then we could have delivered it to the person to whom it was directed. That, at any rate, could surely not have been the wrong thing to do!'

'Well, for my part,' said Miss Ellis, emphatically, 'I am very glad to be rid of it, for now we can forget the whole disturbing business. And as the missing guide book has been returned to us, things are exactly as they were when we started out.'

Elizabeth sighed, and lapsed into silence, watching the gentle rise and fall of the Downs as their chaise travelled along the twisting road which led towards Crowle and the sea. She could not agree with her friend. Nothing could be quite the same again. Robert Farnham had been absent from her thoughts for many years but now she had met him once more, and in a manner that was likely to keep him in her mind for some time; for he was the centre of a mystery that would continue to intrigue her until she had succeeded in solving its riddle. And as it did not seem very likely that she would ever have an opportunity of doing so, now that the packet had vanished and they were leaving the White Hart and its mysterious guests behind, she feared there must be many moments when thoughts of him would intrude on her peace.

She had just finished telling Miss Ellis of her adventures on the preceding night. In the cold light of day, they sounded incredible, and Margaret had been frankly astounded. Elizabeth reflected that perhaps the most incredible thing of all was the fact that she had submitted to a search of her baggage. True, Robert Farnham could have forced her to this; but she had raised no more than a feeble objection, torn between feelings of indignation at being mistrusted and a strong persuasion that he had some legal right to act as he did. She had been spared any embarrassment by the matter-of-fact way in which he conducted the search. It occupied a very short time, and afterwards he had prowled swiftly and efficiently round her room in a practised manner, uncovering hiding places which would scarcely have occurred to her to use, had she been as guilty as he evidently supposed.

He registered no emotion of any kind on finding that she had spoken no less than the truth when she said that the packet had gone. It did not induce him to relax his suspicious attitude towards her, nor to offer any explanation of the mysterious events in which she had been an unwilling participant. Some explanation she had naturally demanded but he had smiled at her cynically, and wished her good night as blandly as if their meeting had been the most ordinary occurrence in the world.

'He is evidently a most unconventional gentleman,' pronounced Margaret disapprovingly, on hearing this. 'And I cannot help feeling, my love, that you had a fortunate escape earlier in life, in not becoming his wife. Besides, whatever his concern in this strange affair may be — whether legal or not — it wouldn't have been at all comfortable for you to have a husband whose occupation in life was of such a nature! There are worse fates, indeed, than that of being a spinster.'

The dark, disturbing presence of Robert Farnham took possession of Elizabeth's senses for a moment. She shivered a little, and shook off the memory, directing her companion's attention to the beauty of the Downland scenery through which they were passing.

It was almost noon when they came to Crowle, a pleasant village with cottages grouped around a green at one corner of which stood the Martlet Inn, a low-lying flint building dating from the fifteenth century, with small latticed windows which glinted in the sun. A small group of men seated outside the tavern on upturned barrels turned to stare at the post chaise as it passed.

'I dare say they don't see many carriages come this way,' remarked Margaret Ellis. 'Oh, dear, how dangerous this road is! I wish the postilion will not go so fast!'

The road along which they turned after leaving the village wound its way around the side of a hill, and was both stony and narrow. The ladies received a severe jolting for the next half-mile or so; until the postilion turned off into an even narrower lane and was obliged to slow the horses to a walking pace, as the high hedges which bordered the lane had not been cut back for some time. At length the chaise passed through the open gates of Crowle Manor, and along a well-kept carriage drive which led straight to the stables. Just before they came to the stable buildings, the drive branched off to the right and brought them to an ornate iron gate set in a high wall which completely surrounded the house.

Miss Ellis peered with some interest through the front window of the post chaise. A circular drive with a plot of grass in the centre fronted the house, and this seemed to be the only stretch of open ground within the encircling wall; for the rest was so thickly covered with trees and bushes that the house seemed almost smothered by them. To add to this effect, the hill which their road had followed rose steeply behind the Manor, shutting off a good deal of light from it. Miss Ellis had too much Yorkshire common sense to follow Anne Horley's example in saying with a shudder that she could never live here; but she could not help feeling that Crowle Manor was decidedly a residence for the summer months only.

The modern frontage with its white stucco and pillared portico somewhat reassured Margaret, as did the appearance of the housekeeper, Mrs. Wilmot, in a respectable grey cotton gown and spotless white cap. The facade turned out to be the only modern feature of the house, however. It had been added by a previous owner to the original Tudor building, and the only benefit it conferred inside was that all the rooms at the front had sash windows which let in a little more light than the tiny casements which appeared elsewhere in the building. As Mrs. Wilmot conducted them upstairs to their bedchambers so that they might remove the dust of travel, Margaret took note of narrow staircases and doorways, and dim, panelled rooms with low ceilings.

'I should imagine you will be at a great expense here with candles,' she remarked to the housekeeper. 'The house is so shut in, darkness must fall early.'

''Tis no great trouble to us, ma'am,' replied Mrs. Wilmot, with a smile. 'Wilmot and me go early to our beds, and there's no one else stays in the house of a night. Unless it might be, ma'am,' she finished, turning now to Elizabeth, 'that mayhap ye'll be wanting to hire a lady's maid to do for ye, seeing ye didn't bring one down from London. If so, there's a female in the village I could recommend, even though she be a Frenchie, and mighty finical in some of her ways.'

'A Frenchwoman?' queried Elizabeth, with interest. 'What is she doing here, then, since we are at war with France? Unless, of course,' she added with a smile, 'she is an emigrée.'

Mrs. Wilmot nodded. 'That's it exactly ma'am. So she be — leastways her father was, so I'm told. But she's been lady's maid to some of they fine Lunnon families until she took ill and came here to get stout again by the seaside — which she's

110

done, now, I hear and anxious to go back to work. So if ye should be thinking of anyone, ma'am —'

Elizabeth looked doubtfully at her friend. 'What do you think, Margaret? For my part, I cannot see the need. We mean to live quietly here, with little or no entertaining — and we can always contrive to do each other's hair. There would be nothing for her to do.'

'Perhaps not; but recollect that I shall not always be with you, as I have promised to give some time to my cousin Ernestine in East Bourne. While I am away, you may be glad of someone else in the house, particularly in the evenings,' replied Margaret, with a doubtful glance about her.

'Well, we will consider it,' conceded Elizabeth, 'and let you know later, Mrs. Wilmot. What a pretty room!' she added, as the housekeeper showed her into one of the bedrooms at the front of the house.

It was indeed a pleasant room, with its gay chintz hangings and soft rose-coloured carpet, and the sunlight striking through the window relieving the heavy effect of the oak panelled walls.

'I'm glad ye're pleased with it, ma'am. The master — that's to say, Mr. Thorne, your late uncle — wasn't much of a one for new furnishings, but he had this room done up six years ago. We did wonder at the time, Wilmot and me,' she added, half-apologetically, 'if the master might have some thought of marriage in his head, for this room was done more in a lady's taste than the rest; but nothing came of it.' Elizabeth reflected that it had been six years ago when Uncle Giles had attended her parents' funeral, and had issued his spontaneous invitation to herself to come and live with him if ever she should feel the need to escape from her close relatives. Could he have returned to his home and deliberately prepared a room for her against the time when she might accept that invitation? It certainly looked very much like it, she thought. What a strange man he had been!

'Was my uncle much in the habit of entertaining friends?' she asked the housekeeper suddenly. She knew quite well he had never been in the habit of entertaining relatives.

It seemed to Elizabeth that for a second a guarded look came over Mrs. Wilmot's face.

'We-ell, ma'am, not to say in the habit. But from time to time the master's friends would drop in, so to speak, and oftentimes when he was away from home, too, though they never stayed above a night or two —'

'You mean to say,' interrupted Miss Ellis, in astonishment, 'that your late master's visitors would stay here in his absence?'

'Oh, yes, ma'am, to be sure. Mr Thorne was a very easy-going gentleman, ma'am, and wouldn't hardly have objected to half the neighbourhood sharing his house.'

'Well!'

'You see, Margaret,' remarked Elizabeth with a smile. 'I have not been the only eccentric in my family.'

Miss Ellis replied that she hoped her young friend's eccentricity would never take quite such an inconvenient form. The housekeeper then showed her to her own bedchamber, which was across the passage from Elizabeth's, and said that a meal was awaiting the ladies when they should be ready for it.

The rest of the day passed away pleasantly enough in settling themselves into their new home. An old-fashioned harpsichord was discovered in the drawing-room, and found to be tolerably well-tuned. A library that was small by the standards of both ladies turned out, on closer examination, to contain a wide selection of reading, and promised many hours of pleasure.

'But I must not do too much reading,' said Elizabeth. 'Recollect that I came here to write.'

'Well, I may read while you go on with your writing,' stated Miss Ellis. 'And I'm sure we shall pass many pleasant days in that way, one each side of the fireplace. Silent companionship, my dear Elizabeth, is as valuable as the more talkative kind. But I'm sure I do not need to tell *you* that.'

As things turned out, the contemplative days which Miss Ellis pictured were destined to remain for the most part a figment of fancy.

Chapter XIII: A Walk by the Sea

The first few days passed peacefully enough. They awoke to a morning of brilliant sunshine, and after taking a leisurely breakfast in an oak-panelled parlour which looked out on to beds of flowers, decided to go for a walk.

Miss Ellis suggested that they might explore the grounds of the Manor, which were fairly extensive; but Elizabeth had set her heart on walking down to the sea.

'It is not very far — less than a mile, I know,' she said, eagerly. 'And Mrs. Wilmot can tell us the way.'

The housekeeper, when questioned, did not recommend the plan. No, it was not far to the cliffs, to be sure; they need only continue along the road they had travelled in the post chaise yesterday. But the road was very stony and rough for a lady's lightly shod feet, and after some distance it deteriorated into a mere track, which petered out altogether as one approached the cliffs, leaving no alternative but to scramble through gorse and bramble.

'And there be nettles a-plenty,' she finished, warningly. 'But doubtless, ma'am, ye'll go no farther than the end of the track, for ye'll have a fine view of the sea from there, and no one wants to go too near the cliff edge, for fear of a fall. Besides, I doubt if the weather will hold for long.'

'Is there nowhere at all near here where we can get down close by the sea?' asked Elizabeth, in a disappointed tone.

'Only on the west side of the Seven Sisters, ma'am, as they call those cliffs hereabouts,' replied Mrs. Wilmot, with a shake of the head. 'And you'll not be likely to walk that far — 'tis all of six mile, and the wind blowin' in your face all the way, for it comes mostly from the west.'

'There's only the gentlest of breezes today,' objected Elizabeth.

'Ay, ma'am, but up on they cliffs it blows something shockin', most times.'

'Very true,' put in Miss Ellis, 'and in any event, we are not thinking of a twelve-mile walk, I imagine. So you see, Elizabeth, we shall have to content ourselves with viewing the mighty ocean from a safe distance.'

Elizabeth was disappointed, but privately determined that she at least would take her view of the sea looking down from as near the cliff edge as possible. Bearing in mind what they had been told of the roughness of the route and the possibility of a boisterous wind, they changed their kid sandals for half-boots, and carried light wool shawls which could be worn for extra warmth if necessary.

The first part of their walk was certainly rough under foot, and with the sun beating down upon them and the hill, sheltering them from the breeze, they began to feel decidedly warm. Miss Ellis murmured something about turning back, but just then they rounded the hill and caught their first view of the sea. Elizabeth exclaimed in delight, and her companion realised that nothing would persuade her to return until they had approached as close to it as possible.

Soon afterwards, the stony road dwindled into a rough track which took a slightly more westerly direction in a valley between rising ground on either side. Gorse bloomed on the hillsides, and a profusion of small flowers made a patchwork of colour. Elizabeth sniffed the air with appreciation, and the scent of wild thyme came to her nostrils, overlaid by the sharper tang of ozone. Ahead, over the cliff, a seagull swooped, the sun glinting on its wings.

'Isn't it beautiful, Margaret?' she said, a little breathlessly. 'Well worth the effort of walking on such a warm day, don't you agree? And it's not so very warm now we are close to the sea.'

'No, indeed, there's quite a fresh breeze, and one or two clouds coming up,' replied Miss Ellis, looking back at the sky. 'I fancy we should do well to turn back now, for fear of being caught in a shower! It is never a good sign when a morning starts off quite so brightly, you know.'

'Well, this is as far as the track goes,' said Elizabeth who was slightly ahead, 'but it's only a little way to the top of the cliff, and, see, there are plenty of places where others have been here before us. The grass is short and does not look at all damp. You need have no fear of getting your feet wet. Why, who would want to build a hut here?'

She broke off as she observed a small wooden hut slightly to westward, at a point where the high cliffs dipped briefly before rising again steeply on the other side.

'Why, see, Margaret, there is a gap in the cliffs!' she exclaimed, excitedly. 'Perhaps we may find a way down to the sea over there!'

Without waiting to hear what her companion thought of this idea, she set off briskly in the direction of the hut. Margaret unfolded her shawl and tied it securely about her shoulders before following. The wind had freshened, and the sky, so blue only ten minutes since, was rapidly clouding over. The ground sloped steeply towards the gap, and both ladies had to take care not to lose their footing. Margaret Ellis privately wondered if her friend had taken leave of her senses to be scrambling about in this way; but she held her peace, recognising that the difference in their ages might account for much.

The slope gradually eased until they were walking over flat ground towards the hut, which was quite close to the cliff edge.

'It looks like a fisherman's hut,' remarked Elizabeth, pausing just before they reached it to don her shawl. 'Would fishermen take out boats from a spot like this, do you suppose?'

'I should think it unlikely — they like a safe harbour,' said Margaret, doubtfully. 'But I am by no means an expert on such matters. Well, here it is at last, and I hope you are satisfied, Elizabeth.'

There was nothing remarkable about the hut. It appeared to be fairly new, and had a door in the side which faced landward, but no window. Elizabeth soon lost interest in it and moved on towards the edge of the cliff. Margaret called out to her sharply to take care, but, seeing this advice went unheeded, she hurried forward herself. Presently they were standing side by side staring down at the narrow strip of shingle and sand which fringed the white-capped waters of the English Channel.

'It's not very high just here, but there's no way down,' said Elizabeth, in a disappointed tone. 'If only we had a ladder, Margaret!'

'For my part, it would make no difference. My days for climbing ladders have long been past — not that it was ever a pastime to which I was particularly addicted. And for the life of me, I cannot see any advantage in our being down below on that strip of shingle, which may soon be completely covered by the incoming tide! Our view of the sea is no less pleasant from here.'

'I would like to bathe in it,' said Elizabeth, wistfully.

Miss Ellis jumped. 'I beg your pardon? *Bathe* in it, did you say? Whatever can have given you such an extraordinary notion? I must say, Elizabeth, you do not seem at all yourself today.'

'Perhaps I am not myself — or perhaps I am myself for the first time in years.'

Miss Ellis studied her in silence for several moments. The sea breeze had whipped colour into her cheeks, deepening the blue of her eyes, and giving her a look of animation which had been missing for some time past. Margaret's expression changed to one of affection. Let Elizabeth indulge her whims, by all means; she had been long enough studying the whims of others. Perhaps here in Sussex she could recover some of her lost youth. There was this Mr. Farnham, too — strange that she should have met him again, although in circumstances which were scarcely conducive to a renewal of his addresses. Miss Ellis sighed; sometimes one did not quite know what to hope for. She would like to see her ex-pupil happily married; but Mr. Farnham appeared to be engaged in an occupation which required him to behave in such an odd manner, that happiness in matrimony would be most unlikely.

She was recalled from her reflections by feeling several spots of rain on her face.

'There!' she exclaimed in vexation. 'I thought we should be caught in a shower! Now what are we to do? There is no shelter anywhere near!'

Elizabeth started to say that she did not think the rain would be very heavy, but changed her mind as the spots increased rapidly, and instead looked about her for some kind of cover.

There was only the hut. Looking at it from the cliff edge, she now noticed that there was a small window in it on the seaward side. Her glance sharpened; surely she had seen a face looking out from the window, hastily withdrawn as she had turned her head in that direction?

'I believe there's someone in the hut, Margaret,' she said, taking her companion's arm and turning away from the cliff edge. 'Let's beg shelter there.'

'What makes you think so? Oh, I see — there is a window, after all. But I can't see anyone there.'

'I'm sure there was someone a moment since, though. We will try, at any rate.'

They hastened to the hut and knocked on the door.

No one answered. Elizabeth knocked again. The rain was coming on faster now, and she flung her shawl over her head to protect her straw bonnet.

'It's no use,' said Miss Ellis. 'The best thing we can do is to stand against the wall on our left. The rain is blowing from the other direction, and we may be partly sheltered from the worst of it. Come along.'

'No, wait, Margaret! Let's try the door first.'

'It's no use — look, there's a padlock.'

'But it's unfastened,' pointed out Elizabeth putting her hand on the padlock, then raising the latch.

The door opened without any trouble and Elizabeth entered. After a moment's hesitation, Margaret followed. A gust of wind swept the rain inside, so she hastily closed the door after her.

It was gloomy inside, and it took a few moments for their eyes to adjust to the poor light provided by the small window looking out on a grey, rainswept sea and sky. When they became more used to it, they peered curiously about them. There was a clutter of gear heaped against the walls of the hut, leaving the middle of the floor clear so that it was possible to walk unimpeded towards the window. This they did, and for a few minutes stood huddled together at the window watching the dismal scene outside.

'I felt sure I saw someone here,' said Elizabeth. 'It's odd, there's no other door than the one we came in by, and we should have seen anyone using that.'

'I dare say it was fancy,' replied Miss Ellis, in a tone of dismissal. 'But I do not feel altogether easy at being here, Elizabeth. We are committing a trespass.'

'Pooh, where's the harm? After all, we had no other shelter from the storm, and the door was open. Oh!' she broke off suddenly, turning towards her companion.

'What is it?' demanded Miss Ellis.

'Why, Margaret, the door was open! And since it is provided with a padlock, doesn't that prove that someone else had come in here before us?'

Miss Ellis shook her head. 'Not necessarily. People do forget to lock doors behind them, you know.'

'Perhaps so. But I am positive,' insisted Elizabeth stubbornly, 'that I did see a face looking out from this window.'

'Well, if so, my dear, it must have been a ghost, for it has vanished into thin air.'

'I suppose,' said Elizabeth, lowering her voice, 'no one could possibly be concealed behind all the clutter against the wall?'

'Only a dwarf, for it does not reach more than a few feet from the ground,' pointed out Miss Ellis dryly.

Undeterred by this remark, Elizabeth moved over to each side of the hut in turn, peering behind thick coils of rope, oars, planking and other odds and ends which were stacked there.

After a time, she turned away, satisfied that no one could be concealed in the hut, and raised her hands to lift down an object which she had noticed hanging from a hook on the wall.

'What do you suppose this can be, Margaret?' she asked, carrying it over to the window. 'It looks like some kind of watering-can — ah, no, I believe it is a curious kind of lantern.'

She held the object up for Miss Ellis to inspect. It was undoubtedly a lantern with sliding shutters which could be adjusted to obscure the light wholly or partially; but its most unusual feature was a spout which was attached to it of some eighteen inches in length and tapering towards the end. 'Well, it is certainly a lantern,' affirmed Margaret, moving the shutters so that the socket for a candle was revealed. 'But I have never in my life seen one similar. Now, what could the purpose of this spout be?' she added, half to herself. 'Supposing one closed all the shutters, the light would appear only as a fine beam through the spout. I cannot imagine any circumstances in which that would be useful can you?'

Elizabeth pondered for a moment with a frown. 'Yes!' she burst out suddenly, in an excited tone. 'Yes, I can, Margaret! What if someone wished to stand on the cliffs, and throw a beam of light down below, or out to sea, without the risk of being seen from inland?'

'My dear Elizabeth! Who in the world would want to do so?'

'Smugglers! They must signal, you know, to those who are waiting at sea in boats, to let them know when it's safe to land! This lantern would be the very thing for that!'

'Smugglers?' repeated Miss Ellis, in tones of derision.

'You are not going to pretend, Margaret, that they don't exist? Why, when we were travelling in the Mail coach, you yourself mentioned how Customs officers sometimes search the coaches for contraband.'

'Well, of course they exist; but I see no reason for supposing that they exist here, just because we have come across a rather uncommon lantern.'

'But it's not only that,' went on Elizabeth. 'What is the purpose of this hut, in so remote a spot? I feel confident that no one would fish from here, for, as you yourself, said, there is no harbour — but I can imagine many ways in which a hut at this point could be very useful to smugglers!'

'My dear, you can always imagine things.'

'You thought I was imagining things about that letter, didn't you, but there turned out to be substance in *that*, at any rate,' retorted Elizabeth, with satisfaction. 'And there are one or two other little points I've noticed to lend colour to this notion of mine: did you not remark only this morning on the very superior brand of tea that Mrs. Wilmot uses? And did you notice how evasive she was when you asked her where she bought it? Oh — and why did she try to put us off taking a walk in this direction?'

'You're surely not going to suggest that the poor woman is hand in glove with a gang of smugglers?'

Elizabeth hesitated. 'Not hand in glove, precisely, but she may know about them. After all, she has lived in these parts all her life, and people take smuggling more or less for granted, don't they? I've heard Philip talking on this subject, and he says that sometimes whole villages get their living by it, just as if it were an honest trade.'

'That may be, but I still think you are erecting too great a structure on a very small foundation — the finding of this lantern,' stated Margaret Ellis, sensibly. 'And therefore, my love, I suggest you hang this up again where you found it, and forget about the whole. See, the rain has stopped, and the clouds are clearing. We shall be able to return soon, though I fear we shall have a very wet and dirty walk back.'

So they did; but at the end of it they were not nearly so wet as the man who had followed them all the way from Crowle Manor and been obliged to crouch in the rain against the side of the hut, while they were sheltering inside. He, too, would have liked to investigate the interior; but this he promised himself he would do another time, when one of his helpers was keeping an eye on the activities of the two ladies. For the present, his duty was clear; he must follow them back again to Crowle Manor. He was satisfied that they had met no one. If they were still in possession of the letter, there had so far been no opportunity for them to hand it over to anyone else.

Chapter XIV: Miss Thorne Engages a Maid

When they reached home, Mrs. Wilmot exclaimed at their soaked footwear and mud-splashed gowns.

'I would have sent one of the lads after you when it came on to rain, ma'am, but there's no taking any vehicle but a farm cart along that track, and 'twouldn't hardly have been any use to you, being as they're so dirty inside, and haven't no cover. And it came down so heavy, too! You must have been soaked, poor ladies!'

'Oh, no,' said Elizabeth, 'we were able to take shelter in the hut that stands near the gap in the cliffs. We weren't outside in the rain for more than a minute or two.'

'Hut, ma'am?' asked Mrs. Wilmot vaguely. 'Well, I'm glad you didn't have to walk through the worst of it, I must say.'

'Do you know the hut I mean?'

'I'm not sure that I do, ma'am; but then I never goes down that way. I gets enough walking round the house and grounds here at home; and an occasional jaunt down to the village, or at times to East Bourne or Seaford in the gig, is all the outings I ask for,' replied Mrs. Wilmot, virtuously seeming to imply that there was the devil's work in walking for its own sake.

'But you must have heard someone mention it, even if you never go there,' persisted Elizabeth. 'What is it used for, do you know?'

'I can't rightly say, I'm sure, ma'am. But hadn't you best change your clothes, for it won't do to be standing about in wet garments — you'll catch your death of cold.'

'Mrs. Wilmot is right, Elizabeth. We should change immediately,' put in Margaret.

'I'll have the hot water sent up to your rooms at once, ladies. I'll just see the kitchen maid about it,' said Mrs. Wilmot, bustling out of the room.

'There! You see,' whispered Elizabeth, as they took their way upstairs.

'See what?'

'How evasive she was! She would not answer my questions at all.'

'I think you refine too much upon too little. She is a very simple kind of character, who always uses a great many words to say what she means, and loses the point of it in the process,' explained Miss Ellis.

'Perhaps. And perhaps it is simply her way of avoiding awkward questions. I don't believe she's nearly as simple as she would have us think.'

After they had bathed and dressed, they went down to the parlour to eat a meal of cold meats and fruit that had been appetisingly set out for them. All the indoor servants came in from the village by day, returning to their homes at night. A few outdoor staff had quarters near the stables, but Mr. and Mrs. Wilmot were the only ones to sleep in the house itself. Wilmot performed the duties of butler; he waited on them at table, aided by a young footman in a rather shabby blue livery.

'There is nothing to complain of in the arrangements here at all,' remarked Miss Ellis, when they had finished their meal. 'The household is well ordered. The only question is whether you would prefer to have one or two of the abigails sleeping in the house.'

Elizabeth replied that she could see no reason for this, and that the present arrangements suited her very well. They returned to the subject a short while later, when Mrs. Wilmot presented herself to say that she had forgotten to mention that the lady's maid she had recommended to Miss Thorne had called that morning while they were out.

'I hope I didn't do wrong, ma'am, but I told her that mebbe you would see her this afternoon,' she concluded. 'If you don't want her, think no more of it; but if you do, I could send down to the village for her to come up whenever you wish, Miss Thorne. 'Tis only a step.'

Elizabeth and Margaret exchanged glances.

'There's your gowns, now, that you got so muddied this morning,' went on Mrs. Wilmot, more boldly. 'Of course, one of the girls can wash and iron them, doubtless, but they won't get them up like Claudette would, her being used to dainty work, as you might say. She looks after a lady as a lady wishes to be looked after, if you take my meaning ma'am.'

After she had gone, they debated the point without any strong interest in it. Miss Ellis tended on the whole to favour engaging a lady's maid, while Elizabeth was totally indifferent. In the end, they decided that there could be no harm in seeing the woman.

'Mrs. Wilmot is evidently very set on finding her a post,' remarked Elizabeth. 'I wonder why?'

'She may have done your housekeeper a kindness at some time or other, or there may be some family connection,' suggested Margaret. 'I don't think we should allow that to set us against her. Of course, you will want other references besides Mrs. Wilmot, who may well be — and most likely is, for one reason or another — biased in her favour.'

But Claudette Faubourg, when she came, brought excellent references from two unquestionable sources, known to both ladies by repute. She was a short, square woman in her middle forties, with a shrewd eye and delicate hands with long, artistic fingers which seemed to belie the rest of her appearance. Her manner was respectful in the extreme, and Elizabeth's only doubt was whether she would grow tired of its sycophantic overtones.

She mentioned this to Margaret when the maid withdrew at last to await their decision.

'Well, I don't know, my love,' said Miss Ellis doubtfully, 'It is the kind of manner which one frequently sees in females who are obliged to earn their own living, towards those whom they hope may be induced to offer them a post. In short, once you have engaged her — if you mean to do so — she may lose that rather tiresomely ingratiating way. I think she would be excellent at keeping your clothes in good order. She has the hands of an artistic person, and is praised for being good with her needle.'

Her friend's remark about the necessity of Claudette Faubourg's earning a living worked on Elizabeth's compassion, always readily aroused, and in the end she decided to engage the woman. It was settled that she should begin her duties that same afternoon, as there was nothing to hinder her.

The weather was so unsettled for the rest of the day that there could be no thought of going out of doors again. The two ladies spent a pleasant hour with the harpsichord, Margaret accompanying while Elizabeth sang some old favourites in her soft, pleasant voice. When they tired of this pastime, Elizabeth fetched the manuscript of her novel and sat down to write, while Miss Ellis occupied herself with her embroidery.

At first, Elizabeth found it difficult to settle to her task. Her story was slight, and relied chiefly on the development of character rather than on such melodramatic incidents as could be found in the pages of Mrs. Radcliffe. She always found it difficult to resume the story after a long interval spent from it, and for the next half-hour or so fidgeted, now mending her pen, now writing a few lines and crossing them out again, in a way that Miss Ellis privately found irritating.

'You do not seem to be going on very well,' she remarked at last.

Elizabeth sighed. 'No. It's always the same when I've neglected my writing for some time. It takes a while, you know, to establish the rhythm, to put myself into the minds of my characters again. But presently I shall re-enter this world of my fancy, and then you will find me reluctant to lay aside my pen for anything.'

She soon proved her point by settling down to composition in earnest, and wrote for the rest of the day without interruption except for meals.

The next morning was bright again, and after breakfast Elizabeth suggested that they should venture out for a while.

'Are there plenty of paths about the grounds?' she asked Mrs. Wilmot. 'The grass will be damp after all the rain we had yesterday, I fear.'

Mrs. Wilmot pursed her lips. 'Not to say plenty, ma'am. There's a wide path takes you from the stables through the trees to the back gate, and a couple of smaller ones leading off it to the different outbuildings. It would be pleasant in the walled garden, though maybe you'll not care to sit in the arbour, for fear of spoiling your dresses. And talking of that, ma'am, Claudette has got your gowns up real fresh and nice again, after all they went through yesterday, you'll be pleased to know.'

Elizabeth made a suitable reply, but she was not particularly in charity with her maid at present, as Claudette had so far shown an irritating tendency to hover about her new mistress.

'It is a good fault, after all,' Miss Ellis had remarked, when Elizabeth complained of it. 'Better than never being able to find her when you require her services.'

They strolled around the walled garden, where roses were in bloom, and then took the winding pathway through the trees which Mrs. Wilmot had mentioned.

'There is plenty of ground here,' remarked Margaret, 'and yet one has the feeling of being shut in — isolated from the outside world. I suppose it's the effect of the hill which rises behind the house. On a dark day, it must be rather melancholy, as your sister Anne remarked.'

'But not on a day of bright sunshine such as this. Besides, I don't mind being isolated for a time — I shall go on all the better with my writing. And we don't appear to have any near neighbours, so there won't be any duty calls to be received or given. That suits my present mood; and when I tire of solitude, I shall return to London, or go and visit one of my friends or relatives.'

Just then, they heard the sound of hoofs approaching along the path, and soon a rider rounded a bend and came into view, taking his horse at an easy trot in the direction of the house.

'You spoke too soon,' said Margaret, with a laugh — 'Here comes someone to call.'

'It must be someone who's very much at home here, then, for he comes by the back way. I dare say it's only one of the stable boys.'

They drew to one side to allow the horseman to pass; but well before he reached them, he swung off the path, taking his way through the trees which soon hid him from view.

Elizabeth halted and turned to stare after him.

'Curious, my love?' asked Miss Ellis. 'Well, it's no use standing there, for there's nothing to be seen of him now. As you said, I expect it was someone from the stables.'

Elizabeth remained in the same attitude and made no reply. 'What are you staring at?' demanded her companion. 'Is something amiss?'

'I don't know,' replied Elizabeth, slowly, starting to walk on again. 'Margaret, did you recognise that rider?'

'Recognise him? How could I? He was too far away to see clearly. Besides, we don't know all the staff as yet. Why do you ask? Did you recognise him?'

'I'm not sure — I only caught a glimpse, but I thought I did.' She paused. 'I thought it was the man Potts — the pedlar who was at the White Hart in Lewes.'

Miss Ellis started. 'Oh, no! Surely not! You could be mistaken — he was not close enough for anyone to be sure.'

'No, that's true. But it's a face I shan't forget — He threw a look at us as he turned off the path — I think he turned off because we were there, and he recognised us.'

'Oh, dear! I thought all that unpleasant business was over and done with — but you may be mistaken, my dear. I defy anyone to be certain of recognising a person at that distance; and we only caught a quick glimpse of him, after all, before he was lost in the trees.'

'Well, we can soon find out,' said Elizabeth, turning on the path. 'We'll return to the house, Margaret, and see if he's there. We shall only be a quarter of an hour at most behind him — and it must take him longer than that to transact any business he has there.'

They retraced their steps, keeping a smart pace back to the house, which they had left some way behind them. As they passed the stables, they looked about them for any sign of the horse or its rider, but saw only a man and a boy cleaning down the stable yard. Elizabeth paused a moment to ask them if anyone had recently come riding up to the house.

'Nobbut the post boy, ma'am,' replied the man.

'Of course!' exclaimed Margaret, in relief, as they crossed the drive to enter the gate that led to the house. 'That would be who our horseman was, without a doubt. You see, Elizabeth, you were letting your imagination run away with you again. I wonder if there will be a letter for me from Cousin Ernestine? I told her to write here and let me know when she would like me to go and visit her.'

They were met in the hall by Mrs. Wilmot, who held up a letter. 'For you, Miss Ellis.'

Margaret took it from her, and glanced at the handwriting on the cover. 'Ah, it is from Ernestine, I see. If you'll forgive me, my dear. I'll read it straight away.'

She took her letter into the parlour, but Elizabeth detained Mrs. Wilmot in the hall for a moment.

'Have there been any visitors while we were out?' she asked.

'Visitors, Miss Thorne? No, ma'am. If there had been, I would have sent after you to fetch you back. Why, were you expecting someone, ma'am? I did not know that you had any acquaintances in this neighbourhood.'

'I only wondered — we passed a horseman coming from the back entrance towards the house, but I did not see clearly who it was, and thought it might have been someone for myself or Miss Ellis.'

'No one's been here, ma'am.' Mrs. Wilmot waited a moment, but Elizabeth said nothing. 'Will there be anything else, Miss Thorne?'

'No, that will be all. Ah, just a moment, Mrs. Wilmot — do you know anybody here by the name of Martin?'

She asked the question on impulse; for a moment it seemed to her that it took the housekeeper aback, for Mrs. Wilmot stood staring at her without attempting to answer.

'Pardon, madam, but which gown will you be wearing for dinner?'

A soft, apologetic voice at her side made her turn away from the housekeeper. The maid Claudette had come quietly downstairs and was standing at her elbow.

'Don't bother me with that now.' Elizabeth's voice was impatient, for her. 'I am talking to Mrs. Wilmot.'

Claudette quickly begged pardon, and, with one brief glance at the housekeeper, withdrew.

'Well,' repeated Elizabeth, 'do you know anyone of that name?'

'I can't say as I do, ma'am,' replied Mrs. Wilmot, her brow furrowed in thought.

'A Mr. Martin — Mr. J. Martin,' Elizabeth persisted.

The housekeeper shook her head. 'No, Miss Thorne.'

'You don't suppose your husband would know? It may possibly be one of the staff.'

'That I can tell you, ma'am. There's no one of that name employed here,' replied Mrs. Wilmot, emphatically. 'But I'll ask Wilmot, for sure, and let you know what he says, ma'am. Will that be all now?'

Elizabeth was disappointed, but dismissed her and joined Margaret in the parlour. She found her friend poring over her letter with a worried frown.

'Not bad news, I hope, Margaret?'

'Not very good, my love. Poor Ernestine has had an inflammation of the lungs, and has been in bed for several weeks and is still confined to the house. She sounds quite low in spirits, poor soul, and says how glad she would be to see me.'

'Oh, dear, I am sorry. If you think you should go to her, Margaret, pray do not stay on my account. We shall have time enough to explore the country together when your cousin is recovered.'

'But I cannot leave you so soon, my love! You are scarce settled in here yet — it would be too bad of me!'

'On the contrary, Margaret. I am very well settled in, and my writing will go along famously in your absence, for I shan't have anything to distract me from it,' insisted Elizabeth, with a smile.

'Well, perhaps I could go just for a few days, to cheer her up a little,' said Miss Ellis, dubiously. 'I can return instantly if you should want me, for it's only five or six miles away, and you can always send someone to fetch me.'

'Of course I can,' replied Elizabeth, cheerfully. 'But I cannot see the least need for anything of the kind. You go, Margaret — I know you'll not be easy unless you do. I shall be quite content on my own for a while in such a peaceful spot, with my book for company.'

Chapter XV: The Hut on the Cliff

The light was rapidly fading, grey clouds obscuring the last rays of the setting sun. A breeze had whipped up, bringing a hint of rain with it. The sea slapped rhythmically at the rocks far below, here and there throwing up a fine jet of spray.

A little way back from the cliff top, a man had been crouching for the past few hours in the unfriendly cover of a gorse bush, intently observing through a pair of powerful perspective glasses the entire area surrounding the hut which stood in that isolated spot. As far as he could tell, the hut was empty. No one had come near it throughout his long and somewhat painful vigil.

Now at last he ventured to leave his hiding place, cursing softly as thorns caught at his bare hands. Still keeping a sharp look-out, he made his way to the seaward side of the hut and peered cautiously in through the window.

The light was too poor for much of the interior to be visible, but he could see no traces of occupation. Encouraged by this, he returned to the door, and set himself to the comparatively simple task of picking the lock. He did not relax his vigilance meanwhile.

A grey haze was settling over the landscape, turning trees and bushes into dark shadows and blurring the rise and fall of the hills against the skyline. It was not an evening to invite strollers along the cliffs; anyone abroad must be on business, not pleasure.

It took him only a few moments to unfasten the padlock, and gain an entrance. He closed the door and made his way cautiously over to the window, looking for something to drape over it so that he could make use of the lantern he had brought with him. He saw there was no need; the window was fitted with a wooden shutter, which he closed. He hung his lantern on a hook in the wall, and turned his attention to the contents of the hut.

He found nothing unexpected. The lantern which had intrigued Miss Thorne was of a type which he had seen before in one or two of the isolated spots which from time to time he frequented. He remembered that there had been one at Rye, and that the smugglers whose property it was had given him some assistance in the mission on which he had been engaged while he was there. Undoubtedly this lantern, too, was owned by a gang of smugglers. It was no surprise to him to discover that there was smuggling going on at Crowle, for he had suspected it all along. The suspicion had soon been confirmed on his arrival in the village, when he had tried to find a lodging for himself and his helpers. Not wishing to appear in the public eye himself, he had sent one of his men to make the necessary inquiries. The report indicated that Crowle was an inhospitable place. The Martlet Inn never took in guests, and it seemed that no money could buy a bed for a stranger in any of the village homes. After some trouble, they had found an abandoned cottage in a remote spot about half a mile from the village, and here they made their headquarters. Farnham, however, spent much of his time in the grounds of Crowle Manor, where he found plenty of temporary hiding places in the outbuildings, which were not very much used by the household staff. The two ladies at the Manor had been kept under constant surveillance since their departure from Lewes, so far without result. They had met no one to whom they could have passed on the packet, and Farnham now felt certain that it was not in their possession. That left Mrs. Wood or the pedlar. Mrs.

Wood, he knew, had gone to Brighton, closely attended without her knowledge by another of Farnham's helpers. It seemed most probable that, if she had indeed been involved in the business, her part was now done. For his money, thought Farnham, the pedlar was the man to watch. But where the devil was he? If he had arrived in the village, he was lying very low, for there had been no sign of him so far.

Not for the first time, he speculated about the identity of J. Martin, of Crowle Manor. Tactful and costly investigation had shown that there was no one of that name employed there. Possibly Mr. Martin was an infrequent visitor; smugglers carried more than one kind of cargo from the shores of France. To recover those documents was of the first importance, but it was also essential to put an end to the activities of this unknown gentleman. He frowned. If the pedlar was in possession of the packet, as seemed most likely, the obvious move to make was to track him down and take him into custody. But to do this would be to lose the opportunity of capturing the mysterious Mr. Martin. Sooner or later, the man must come to Crowle Manor, for that, Farnham knew, was the place appointed for these two to meet. By keeping a constant watch on the Manor, it should be possible eventually not only to recover the precious packet but also put both Martin and the pedlar out of what was doubtless a most profitable line of business for them.

Where did Elizabeth Thorne come into all this, he wondered? She could not have been the courier originally charged with the task of conveying the packet from London, or she would have passed it on to Potts at the White Hart without delay once the pedlar had made her aware of his complicity. Yet it had been at one time in her possession, for she had owned as much two nights ago in Lewes, when

Farnham had confronted her in her room. Could she have come by it accidentally? This scarcely seemed feasible, yet more unlikely still was the notion that she had stolen it from Mrs. Wood for reasons of her own. What kind of reasons could there be? Not for the first time he felt that he must have another interview with Miss Thorne.

As these thoughts ran through his mind, he was examining the contents of the hut with all his accustomed thoroughness, moving sundry objects to make quite certain that they concealed nothing of greater interest to him. That was how he came to discover a trap door in the floor, with a round iron handle sunk into a socket in the wood. His glance sharpened. Quickly he cleared the litter from around the door, then, seizing the handle, gave a sharp tug. The trap door opened readily, as though on greased hinges, and he found himself looking down a flight of wooden steps.

He jumped to his feet and seized the lantern from the wall. Adjusting the shutters so that only a glimmer of light would show, he fastened the lantern to a leather strap which he wore about his waist. It was a device which allowed him to have both hands free to deal with any emergency which might arise, and it had stood him in good stead on previous hazardous occasions. Leaving the trap door open, he began to descend the steps.

He had to go very slowly, as the thin light from his lantern did little to dispel the surrounding gloom. The steps appeared to be sturdy, though, and provided adequate footing. As he descended, a dank smell came to his nostrils; and not far off he could hear the hiss and rattle of shingle flung to and fro by the tide. He soon realized that he was going down into a cave which had an outlet to the sea.

When he reached the bottom of the steps, he stood still for a moment, listening for any other sound than that of the sea. Presently, he unhooked his lantern, adjusting it so that it gave full light, and raised it above his head. As well be hanged for a sheep as a lamb, he thought; anyone who was in the cave must already have seen the glimmer of light as he descended. He braced himself for an attack, but none came. Evidently nobody was in the cave at present.

He moved here and there with the lantern, looking curiously about him. It was not a large cave; the staircase descended from its highest point, and elsewhere the height of the roof varied from places where he could stand upright with ease to others where he was obliged to stoop. Several lanterns were suspended from hooks in the walls, and sturdy coils of rope lay on the floor which was dry. Two small rowing boats were beached against one side. Close to these, he found an opening through which grey light filtered. He stooped a little to enter, and found himself in a narrow passage which bent round at an angle before finally emerging beneath an overhang of jutting rock right at the foot of the cliff.

Pausing to close down the shutters of his lantern, he stepped out of the narrow mouth of the passage on to the few feet of rock and shingle which had been exposed by the receding tide. From the decaying seaweed round his feet, he guessed that the sea rarely came up as far as the entrance to the passage; that was why the floor of the cave had been dry. It was twilight now, and he gazed across the grey waters which merged on the horizon into the misty sky. Somewhere across that expanse of restless sea lay the cause of all this trouble. His mouth took on a grim line. He must not loiter here, now that he had seen all there was to see. He still had work to do. He turned, stooping to enter the passage once more, at the same time providing himself with a thin beam of light from the lantern. He was half-way along the passage, just about to round the bend, when he pulled up sharply.

The sound of voices drifted down from the cave.

He closed down the light completely, and drew a pistol from his pocket. It would not suit his plans to shoot anyone at this stage of the business, but he might be forced to do it in self-defence. If these proved to be the smuggling gentry — and who else would be here —? they certainly would not welcome a stranger in their haunts. Already the open outer door and the trap door must have warned them that there was someone here.

He stood still for a moment, listening. Then, as he heard the voices and footsteps coming closer, he changed his mind and pocketed the pistol. If possible, he would avoid a confrontation with the smugglers. But where the devil could he find cover in this spot?

He groped his way back to the beach, relying on his memory for avoiding the hazards of jagged rocks which he had passed before. It was almost dark outside, and a wind was blowing off the sea. If he flung himself flat on the beach against the foot of the cliffs, would he escape notice? A ray of light from the passage warned him that this would be hopeless. He could not go far enough in the time left to him, and their lanterns would soon reveal anyone lurking close at hand.

Desperately his eye searched the cliff face for any sign of a cleft or hole big enough to conceal a man, but he could see nothing of the kind. And then his roving glance fell upon the overhang of rock which partly concealed the entrance to the passage. It sloped forward at a sharp angle from the cliff face, but an active man with strong muscles might manage to cling there for a time. There was no certainty that he could escape notice, even so; if they chanced to look upwards he would be discovered, but it was the best he could do in the time he had.

He gripped the overhang and swung himself up, perching precariously on tiptoe right on the edge. Gradually, he straightened himself, searching for firm hand- and footholds that would enable him to flatten his body against the rock. He managed to achieve this more or less satisfactorily just in time, for at that moment a light appeared beneath him, and two figures stepped out of the passage on to the beach, only a yard or two from where he was perched.

'O' course someone's been here,' growled a voice. 'Why else was the trap open? Tell me that.'

Farnham twisted his head slightly, and saw that two men had come out on to the beach. He recognised the one holding the lantern at once; it was Potts, the pedlar.

'Someone's been here, right enough,' agreed Potts. 'But the question is, has he gone or is he still here? And more than that, who is he and what's he after?'

They walked some distance along the beach in the direction of the Gap. Farnham could see their lantern bobbing to and fro as they searched for him among the rocks which lay scattered at the foot of the cliffs. When he judged they were far enough away, he jumped down from his perch and darted into the passage, flexing his aching muscles.

He approached the cave with caution, uncertain if others might be there; but although he found a lantern burning, the place was empty.

He glanced at the trap door, and saw that it was still open, as he had left it. Soft footed, he climbed the steps and peered cautiously over the top into the hut.

Satisfied that no one was there, he emerged from the opening and crossed quickly to the door. He let himself out, and was about to close the door quietly behind him before making good his escape, when he changed his mind. Instead, he left the door a fraction ajar; not sufficiently, he hoped, to be noticed by anyone inside the hut, but perhaps enough to allow him to see and hear what was happening from outside. He stationed himself against the wall beside the door, and experimentally put his eye to the crack.

The results were disappointing; he could see very little. Nothing daunted, he remained where he was, flattening himself back against the wall.

He was not exactly expecting to see anything of importance; but it was possible that when the men returned to the hut, as they were almost certain to do before long, he might succeed in overhearing something of interest to him. It seemed a reasonable assumption that they had already made a search for him above ground before going down below. They were not likely to do so a second time. Even if they did, it was now dark enough for him to stand a good chance of eluding them on this open ground.

He had not long to wait. Soon he heard the trap door slam and the shuffling of boots on the floorboards of the hut.

'He's cleared off, whoever he was.' The gruff voice carried clearly enough to Farnham's ears. 'Don't like it, though, Jem. There was a cove round the village a couple o' nights since, seekin' a bed. Foreigner, they said, not from these parts by his speech. I'd give a deal to know who 'tis as takes such an interest in our doings.'

'I'm with you there, Reuben.' It was the voice of Potts. 'I bain't superstitious in general, but this business o' mine seemed fated from the start. First of all, that tarnation female who was bringin' me the letter from Lunnon gets the jitters about somethin' that happened on the journey down, and what does she do but shove it in a book belongin' to two other females what was in the coach. A damn silly thing to do, for she might 'ave knowed it was all a fuss over naught, and no end o' trouble to get the letter back again afterwards. But that's women for ye — never trust 'em in business.'

Farnham controlled a start. So that was it! The woman Mrs. Wood had been the courier, after all, and the packet had come into Elizabeth's possession by accident. And he had accused her in such terms — Good God, what must she think of him? Could she ever forgive him? There seemed small chance of it. He brushed aside these disturbing thoughts, and strained his ears to follow the rest of the conversation.

'Ye need a drink, that's what, brother, and I reckon we've earned one, chasing after yon nosey parker. I must be off soon to round up the lads, and get together horses and a cart or two for when the boats arrive. But they'll not come much afore three, so there's plenty o' time for a drop o' grog. I reckon ye're not in a hurry either to get off up to the Manor, as yer man won't be there for long enough. What d'ye say?'

Potts murmured an assent. Presently Farnham heard the gurgle of liquid being poured out, soon followed by a smacking of lips and prolonged sighs of satisfaction.

'Ah, that's better,' remarked Potts. 'But the worst of it was, Reuben, them two females was none other than the two that's come to stay at the Manor. And they found that letter right enough, for they'd put it in another hiding place when that half-witted woman Wood went to try and get it back. No end o' trouble she had; but get it she did at last, though before she brought it to me, someone — and I don't know who, no more than fly in the air — someone comes out to the loft where I'm sleepin', and lays me out, good and proper.'

'Did they, now? Well, might 'ave been a pickpocket, Jem. Ye carry a fair bit o' stuff around in that pack o' yourn — must be a temptation to light-fingered folk.'

'That's what I thought, till I find there's naught missing. But I could tell this cove 'ad been through my pack — ay, and my pockets, too, for all I can tell, though I can't swear to that, for all was in place, just as I'd had it before. But one or two little things was different in the pack, see?'

There was a short silence; evidently Reuben was thinking this over.

'Well, I'll admit it sounds queer,' he said at last. 'But it bain't likely that this cove who's been 'ere tonight is the same as attacked ye at Lewes. Ye'll take another mug, Jem?' Another drink was poured.

'Unless it's the law,' replied Potts, slowly. 'But I can't hardly think they'd go about things in that kind o' way. Besides, who's to know I was here, or to connect us with each other? We take care not to be seen abroad together.'

'Ye takes care,' Reuben reminded him, with a hint of hostility.

'D'ye blame me? It don't do for me to be known as an associate o' smugglers. My business is too ticklish to get mixed up in anything o' that kind.'

Reuben snorted. 'Hark at ye! As though being courier to Monsoor Martin and 'is bunch o' Frogs was a cut above an honest bit o' freebootin', which never hurt nobody.'

'Ye're in that as deep as I am, brother. Ye takes 'em to and fro across the Channel, don't ye?'

'Well, what's it matter?' demanded Reuben, truculently.

'We gets good pay, don't we? Tell me anything else that pays 'alf as well, and I'm yer man for it. Drink up and take another.'

Potts swallowed noisily.

'Oh, ay, ye're in the right of it there, Reuben. No, I don't hardly think it can be the law, nor yet the Customs. D'ye reckon it might be someone put on by them two females at the Manor to find out what goes on here? Ye said they was pokin' about in the hut yesterday.'

'I don't 'ardly think they was pokin' about,' answered Reuben, thoughtfully. 'From what I could see o' them — though I 'ad to duck down below quick — they was just lookin' for somewhere to shelter from the rain, and this was the only place handy. And me havin' left the door unfastened, like a fool, for I'd only slipped in for a few minutes to bring some things for tonight's work.'

'Oh, well, if ye thinks that's all,' Potts said, in relief. 'But I got a turn this morning, I can tell ye — I almost rode into 'em. I avoided the village, same as always when I arrives in daylight, and rode up to the Manor by the back way, thinking to sneak into the hidden room there that Monsoor Martin uses when he's in these parts, the same where I shall 'and over the packet to him tonight. I'm not supposed to go there except by arrangement with him, but I reckon what the eye don't see the 'eart can't grieve over, and it's a fine place to lie low. I intended to stay there until after dark, then go to your place in the village for a bite and a sup, and back again near the time as he's expected to land. He'd never 'ave been any the wiser. But them tarnation females scared me off, so I came 'ere instead.'

'Well, ye knew they was there,' pointed out Reuben reasonably. 'Pity ye didn't come straight to Crowle from Lewes, Jem, then ye'd 'ave been safely tucked away in that hidey 'ole before ever they arrived.'

'I suppose ye'd have come straight to Crowle, would ye?' jeered Potts. 'After what 'appened to me at the White Hart an' all? Well, if so, ye'd be a fool, brother, and not the man for a chancy game such as I plays. No, ye stick to yer smugglin', me lad, and leave the clever one o' the family to work that needs nerve and wits.'

'Clever, eh?' shouted Reuben, bringing his fist down with a thump on something hard. 'I suppose ye don't reckon as it needs nerve and wits to run this freebootin' business, then, eh? Why, ye cocky little bastard, ye, I've a good mind to serve ye as ye was served in Lewes, damn yer eyes!'

Farnham could see that a family quarrel was well under way, aggravated no doubt by the liquor that both men had been imbibing so freely. He wondered if he was likely to learn much more in the circumstances, and was just deciding to leave when a gust of wind caught at the open door and shut it with a slam.

At once he took to his heels, but a crack of light from the door warned him that they were opening it. He flung himself down flat on the ground, thinking that he would more readily escape notice than if he continued to run. By the light from the door, he saw the two men emerge; but evidently they did not wish to show lights on the top of the cliff, for they were not using the lantern, and soon closed the door again.

He waited, motionless, listening for their approach. If they came too close, he must make a dash for freedom, but he would prefer not to disclose his presence if possible.

After a few minutes, the light from the door showed again briefly as the two men went back into the hut. Evidently they were satisfied that no one had been there, and that one of themselves must have been responsible for leaving the door ajar so that it slammed in the wind.

So much the better, Farnham thought maliciously: it would no doubt add fuel to the family squabble that had been brewing previously.

He smiled grimly as he went in search of his horse and took the way back to Crowle Manor.

Chapter XVI: The Secret Agent

An owl's cry sounded from the trees close to the house. Hearing the signal, the watcher turned towards it, joining Farnham in the shadows. For a time the two men talked together in low tones.

'After you've sent Taylor off for the dragoons, return to me here,' instructed Farnham, presently. 'Somehow or other, I must locate this secret room before our friends come to keep their rendezvous. If we try to take them outside, there's a chance that one or other of 'em will get away, with only the two of us. Tell Taylor to ride as if the devil's after him. Now I must find a way in.'

'There's something I spotted earlier on in my watch,' said the other man, pausing as he turned on his heel. 'It looks like a door, but there's no latch that I could find. It's in the side of the house nearest to us, against the chimney, hidden by the creeper that grows there.'

'I'll investigate. Anyone sleep that side of the house?'

'The housekeeper's room is on the other side, at the back. I saw a light there some time back. The abigail's in an attic room, where I can't say.'

'Evidently you're not on form,' jibed Farnham.

The other snorted in disgust. 'The wrong side of forty, and about as cuddlesome as a porcupine! I'll be off, then.'

It was quite dark, for there was no moon, but Farnham approached the house with caution. After two days of constant watch, he knew the terrain well. There was no window at this side of the house, only a blank cream-coloured wall with a chimney running up the centre of it, so there was no danger of being overlooked. He trained a thin beam of light on the area at the base of the chimney.

At first, he could see nothing, so he gently lifted the creeper aside. He found it came quite readily, as though used to such treatment. He played the ray from his lantern over the area underneath, and was able to trace the outline of a narrow panel of wood painted the same colour as the surrounding bricks. It was large enough to admit a man, but there was no way of opening it that he could see.

He ventured to allow himself a little more light, and followed the outline of the door round several times. The last time, he noticed a small indentation low down on the right-hand side, only big enough to take a fingertip. He inserted his index finger, and pressed firmly. There was a slight click, and the door slid back.

He thrust the lantern into the aperture. It was very little wider than the door, and plentifully festooned with spiders' webs. Carefully stepping over the trailing stems of the creeper, he entered and raised the lantern to look about him. The cavity went back only a few feet, and out of it rose a steep flight of wooden steps enclosed by walls on either side.

He nodded: a staircase up the side of the chimney, and no doubt leading to the secret room.

Before mounting the stairs, he stopped for long enough to master the mechanism that controlled the sliding door. He reached out and pulled the creeper back in place before finally closing it. Then he adjusted his lantern to give full light, and turned to climb the stairs.

A man needed to be in condition for this form of exercise, he reflected; if the staircase led to a hiding place that had been used by a priest in the bad old days of religious persecution, then it must be hoped that the priest had not been elderly. But no doubt there would be another way into the secret room from inside the house, and this stairway would have been used chiefly as an exit.

At last the stairs ended abruptly, and he found himself facing another door. This time, his hand quickly found the mechanism that controlled it, and it slid smoothly back. He stepped into the room beyond, closing the panel behind him.

It was a tiny room, scarcely six feet square. Against one wall was a narrow truckle bed with a chair beside it. On the opposite side was a small washstand with a wall cupboard above it. There was another full length cupboard in the wall opposite the entrance to the stairs. There was no door leading out into the house, as far as Farnham could see.

He set his lantern down and inspected the furniture and fittings. He found two packed bags under the bed, but although they held a quantity of male attire, they contained no papers of any kind. Pushing them back, he turned his attention to the washstand and the cupboard above it. Here he found everything a man might need who proposed to camp out in the room for several days. He cast an envious eye on a pie which rested on one of the shelves in the cupboard. Its appetising brown crust tempted him sorely, for he had not eaten for some hours, but he forced himself to resist the temptation. He must leave no sign that anyone else had been here for his quarry to find.

He closed the doors of the washstand and cupboard carefully, and turned to inspect the large cupboard in the other wall. The door opened readily, revealing a small space with a row of hooks along the back wall, presumably for hanging up clothes.

Farnham frowned. If a man had somewhere to hang his clothes, why leave them bundled up in valises under the bed?

So that he could move out quickly, if need be? Possibly; all the same, a clothes cupboard did seem an unnecessary luxury in a hideaway such as this, and surely concealed somewhere in the room must be a way into the main part of the house.

Stepping inside the cupboard, he ran his fingers over the wall at the back, and found that it was no plaster as he had supposed, but wood. After that it took him only seconds to discover that it opened in a similar way to the other two panels through which he had passed.

He snatched up the lantern, and stepping over the threshold of the cupboard, shone his light round the room beyond. He was standing in one of the attics at the back of the house. It was crammed with all kinds of junk — weary armchairs with broken legs and torn upholstery, discarded pictures and ornaments, a battered wooden settle. His eye took in these details before he glanced at the dormer window and cautiously shut down his lantern. The pedlar might arrive at any time, and it would not do for him to see a light in this part of the house. But this cluttered attic would provide splendid cover when the moment came to take him and the spy Martin into custody.

Farnham stepped back into the priest's hole and gave a quick look round to assure himself that nothing showed signs of being disturbed. Satisfied on this score, he returned to the attic, closing both doors of the cupboard behind him. Then he began to thread his way through the clutter of the room towards the door. He had almost reached it when his foot caught in the rocker of a child's wooden cradle, setting it noisily in action. He put out his hand at once to stop it, cursing softly. Reaching the door, he opened it cautiously, and peered round.

He drew back quickly. Farther along the passage, the door of the next room had opened. He had just time to glimpse a woman coming out with a candle in her hand before he softly closed the door and took cover behind the settle. He closed the shutters right down on his lantern and crouched in the darkness, waiting.

After a few moments, he heard the attic door opening, and the woman advanced a little way into the room.

'Is anyone there?' she said, quietly. She did not sound at all alarmed.

She moved forward a few paces, letting the light of her candle play as far as possible round the room. Farnham hoped that she would come no farther. She was only a few yards away from where he crouched, and he had no wish to tangle with a female. It must be Miss Thorne's abigail; she slept in the adjoining room.

She stood there for a little while longer.

'Perhaps it was the cat,' he heard her murmur to herself. 'Silly creature! Come on out, then — puss, puss!'

Farnham heartily wished that he could have conjured up a cat to oblige her, fearing now that she would search the entire room for the fictitious animal. He was beginning to work out a plan of campaign, when she seemed to lose interest, and, with another quick look about her, went out, closing the door.

He waited for some time before he ventured to look out into the passage. It was dark and deserted. Not knowing his way about the house, he risked using the lantern to help him reach the ground floor. His confederate had told him that Miss Thorne was still downstairs in the parlour at the back of the house. She had been busy writing when the curtains had been pulled, so he had said; with any luck, Farnham hoped he might find her there still. He had a great deal to say to her.

Elizabeth had experienced difficulty in persuading Miss Ellis that she might as well depart for East Bourne that same afternoon, but in the end she prevailed. The truth was that authorship had her in its grip. Since her session with her manuscript the previous evening, ideas had come crowding thick and fast into her mind, and she desired nothing so much at present as to be free to take up her pen again without outside distractions. Margaret knew her friend well enough to see how it was, and to feel less compunction than she might have done at leaving her in solitude.

'At any rate, you will have the abigail to bear you company if you wish to go walking,' she said, when it was all decided. 'But I do beg of you, Elizabeth, not to get yourself into any foolish scrapes by letting your fancy run away with you! I shall not stay with Ernestine above three or four days, and you may send for me at any time, you know. Don't hesitate to do so.' She handed her a piece of paper. 'I have written down the direction here for you.'

Elizabeth placed the paper in her writing-case, and promised to do as she was asked. Miss Ellis packed a few things with the minimum of fuss, as was her way, and set out on her short journey early in the afternoon. Soon afterwards, Elizabeth settled down to her writing in the back parlour, and grudged every interruption to it which followed.

There were more than she might have anticipated.

Tea arrived at the usual time and was not unwelcome; but when Mrs. Wilmot came in to clear away, she showed a disposition to chat. Elizabeth had scarcely succeeded in banishing her when Claudette came into the room, with a query as to which gown should be laid out for the evening. Elizabeth started to say that she would not change, as she was to dine alone; but the shocked look on the maid's face made her decide to sacrifice a little time rather than wound such fine susceptibilities. Afterwards, she was glad, for a short while at least, that she had conceded this sartorial point.

'I really do not mind — anything will do,' she stated, pointedly taking up her pen again.

After that, there was peace for an hour or so, until Claudette reappeared, soft-footed as usual, to remind her mistress that it was time to dress unless she wished dinner to be served at a later hour than usual.

'Is it really that time?' asked Elizabeth, glancing at the clock. 'Oh, no, I would not wish to put them to so much trouble in the kitchen — I will come upstairs at once.'

She paused only long enough to tidy her loose papers away in a folder, then rose to follow Claudette, who had already left the room. She was walking along the passage to her bedroom when she noticed Mrs. Wilmot about to ascend the stairs leading to the attic bedrooms. The housekeeper was carrying a tray covered with a cloth, and it appeared to be heavy. She faltered slightly once, and Elizabeth heard the chink of china. She had no time to stop and wonder about this, for Claudette was waiting at the bedroom door and she at once took charge, pouring warm water into the washbasin and afterwards helping Elizabeth out of her gown. She certainly knew how to make one feel comfortable, reflected Elizabeth; but what a pity that she felt it necessary to be always in attendance, as she evidently did. At home, Elizabeth had shared a maid with her sister Anne, and was not at all used to so much attention. She found it irked her, but she was too kind-hearted to show her impatience.

'You look delightful, madam,' remarked Claudette, later, when she was twisting Elizabeth's warm-brown hair into a classical knot on the top of her head.

Elizabeth regarded herself thoughtfully in the mirror. She was wearing a high-waisted gown of blue muslin, embroidered with sprigs of white. Round her neck on a simple gold chain was a blue locket containing a miniature of her mother. Her eyes looked a deeper blue than usual, reflecting the colour of her dress.

'Do I?' she asked, laughing softly. 'If so, it is your doing, and quite wasted, I fear, for no one will see your handiwork.'

She ate her solitary meal and returned to the parlour to resume work on her manuscript. But even now she was not to be free of interruptions, for Claudette, who was sitting in the small ante-room doing some mending, came in several times on errands which seemed to Elizabeth quite unnecessary.

Her final appearance was to bring in the tea-tray at a quarter to ten, announcing that she did so because Mrs. Wilmot had gone to bed.

'And so may you,' Elizabeth told her. 'Your eyes must be quite tired, doing that fine work by candlelight, and I shall not require you any more tonight.'

'But, madam,' Claudette protested, 'I must wait up to help you with your hair.'

'Not at all. I may very well do it myself — indeed, I have mostly been accustomed to. Good night.'

Claudette's expression indicated that this was not at all the kind of thing she had been used to in her previous situations; nevertheless, she was obliged to accept her dismissal. She bade her mistress good night and went away, presumably to gather up her work and go to bed as she was bidden. Elizabeth gave a sigh of relief, drank her tea, and quickly resumed her writing.

Silence crept over the room, broken only by the soporific ticking of the clock and the busy scratching of Elizabeth's pen. An hour passed, and she was far away in the realms of fancy when a slight creak told her that the door was opening. She had her back to it; thinking that Claudette must have returned for some reason, she did not bother to turn round, but told her quite sharply to go away.

The door closed, and she heard a quiet voice behind her say, 'It is not your maid.'

It was Robert Farnham's voice, as she knew at once. She turned sharply, rising from her chair, which would have fallen to the floor with a clatter had he not leapt forward and seized it.

'Don't cry out, I beg you!' he exclaimed, in a low tone, seeing her amazed look. 'I must talk to you, Elizabeth.'

She recovered herself with an effort. 'How — how did you get into the house?' she stammered. 'There's no one to let you in.'

'I let myself in,' he answered, briefly. 'But more of that presently. We're not likely to be disturbed here, are we? You've sent the servants to bed?'

She nodded, watching him without speaking.

'Good,' he said, then hesitated for a moment. 'Elizabeth, I scarcely know how to begin. When we last met, I treated you in such a way, said such things to you — it was all a mistake. Can you possibly forgive me?'

'I'm not sure.' She regarded him gravely.

'I owe you some explanation. Will you allow me to make it, at any rate?'

Her face relaxed into a brief smile. 'Yes,' she replied, honestly, 'because I am so very curious as to what it will be.'

'Then I'll tell you what I can. But a moment — can we be overheard in here?'

He glanced at the ceiling, and she shook her head.

'There is no one in the room above. The housekeeper and her husband have a bedchamber on the other side.'

'And the abigail, I know, sleeps in an attic room,' he said. 'Perhaps it would be as well to make sure that she's not left it.'

He moved quietly to the door and opened it suddenly. He stepped out into the passage, where a light was still burning, and looked up and down for a few moments. Satisfied, he returned to the room and closed the door.

'What's in there?' he asked, pointing to the door of the ante-room.

'A small room where she was sitting sewing before I sent her to bed. You may look there if you wish.'

He took up the candle from the writing-desk, and, pushing open the door, went into the tiny room. It contained only a small table and two chairs. There was another door leading out into the passage. This he had noticed when he had stood in the passage a few moments earlier, so he did not bother to open it. A glance showed him that the room was empty and that it contained no possible hiding place.

'I have to make sure,' he said, as he closed the door of the ante-room behind him and replaced the candlestick on the desk. 'What I have to say is of the utmost secrecy, and for your ears alone.'

'The prospect of hearing it fascinates me,' remarked Elizabeth, with a faint smile. 'Perhaps we had better sit down? I cannot offer you any refreshment, I fear, unless there is some wine in the sideboard —'

He glanced at her quizzically. 'You don't seem unduly shocked at the thought of being closeted with a man at this hour in a house where all the servants are abed?'

'I find it diverting. So very few adventures ever befall me — or at least, that used to be true until very lately. Besides —' she hesitated, and a faint colour came into her cheek — 'we are not quite strangers.'

'No,' he replied, gravely, watching her as she sat down by the fireside, then taking the wing chair opposite her. 'Would you care to tell me about your recent adventures, Elizabeth?'

She raised her eyebrows. 'Did I say you might use my name?'

'May I not?' A keen glance from his dark eyes studied her expression. 'No, I forget, you haven't yet undertaken to forgive me. Very well, Miss Thorne it shall be, then. I beg you, Miss Thorne to tell me everything that's happened to you since you left London, particularly anything connected with the packet that came into your possession, or with the woman known as Mrs. Wood or the pedlar Potts. And, indeed, any other incidents which seem to you strange that have occurred to you here in Crowle.'

'Oh dear! I hope you have plenty of time.'

He nodded. 'At least three or four hours, I think, though I don't propose to inflict myself on you for that length of time, so don't worry. There are things I must do later. But now I would like to hear your side of the story, and then I will tell you mine. Pray begin, ma'am.'

Elizabeth was only too glad to oblige, for she felt that at least there was some hope of her finding the solution to so much that had puzzled her in recent events. Her practice in telling a story stood her in good stead now, and the attention with which Farnham listened while she unfolded the tale would have flattered her extremely had it been one of her own concoction.

He nodded in a satisfied way several times, and interrupted only once. That was when she recounted how she had gone down to the stableyard to try and overhear the conversation between Potts and Mrs. Wood.

'That was very unwise,' he said, gravely. 'These are very dangerous people — don't underrate them. Had they discovered you, they would not stop at murder.'

She shivered. 'I felt that at the time, although I did not know what it was all about. And then, of course,' she resumed, 'I managed to get back to my room and found you there.'

'You can leave that part out,' he said quickly, with a shamed look. 'When I think of what I said to you —! But it was all a misapprehension. I will tell you afterwards, when you have done, and then maybe you can understand, and from understanding perhaps even come to forgive a little — though I realise it's more than I deserve. But I'm distracting you — pray continue with what happened after I left you that night.'

Elizabeth took up the tale with the arrival of Margaret and herself at Crowle Manor, the walk on the cliff and the discovery of the hut, rounding off her account with the glimpse of the horseman that morning, whom she had thought was the pedlar.

'I could not be certain,' she concluded, 'as he was too far away and I only saw him for a moment before he turned off into the trees. Of course Margaret thought I was imagining things again, but I really had a singularly strong impression that it was the man Potts.'

'You were right,' he stated. 'It was. I have just come now from the hut on the cliff — which, as you supposed, is used for smuggling — and I saw the pedlar there with another man, who is evidently his brother and a leading light in the local free-booting business.'

'Smuggling here in Crowle!' exclaimed Elizabeth. 'Do you suppose the Wilmots are involved in it in any way? As I told you, there have been one or two little things which made me wonder —'

'They may or may not be involved in it,' he replied slowly. 'It could be that they benefit by it without taking any active part themselves. Or it could be that they are involved in a far more dangerous game than smuggling — that is something for me to discover if I can.'

She stared at him, 'A more dangerous game? What could that be? It's something to do with the letter, isn't it — the letter to J. Martin, Esq., of Crowle Manor? There's no such person living here, you know. I've asked several people, and no one admits to knowing anyone of that name at all — although I must say Mrs. Wilmot looked a trifle taken aback when I questioned her, as though she knew more than she was prepared to admit.'

'Hm,' he remarked thoughtfully. 'I hope to bring this affair to a successful conclusion tonight, but if the Wilmots are in it, they might well queer my pitch.'

'What *is* your pitch?' asked Elizabeth, her eyes alight with curiosity. 'Are you a Customs officer? You were not, when I knew you first.'

He laughed shortly. 'A Preventive man? Nothing so respectable, Eliz—, Miss Thorne. I am a secret agent for Mr. Canning, the Foreign Secretary.'

Chapter XVII: Return of Love

Elizabeth considered him thoughtfully. He had expected a rather different reaction.

'A secret agent?' she repeated, slowly. 'I'm not sure that I know what that is.'

'I don't suppose you would. It's a euphemism for a rather more ugly word — a spy.'

'A spy!' She echoed the word on a breath of sound, and was silent for a moment, while he watched her. 'I see,' she said, at last, in a different tone. 'I never knew we had any — that is to say, one always supposes that it is the enemy who makes use of spies.'

'We are the enemy to those on the other side of the Channel,' he reminded her.

'I suppose so — yes, of course, I see that it must be just as important for the English government to have information out of France as for Napoleon Bonaparte to find out what is going on over here. But is it not a very dangerous profession?'

He smiled a little more easily. 'Hazardous, yes. But not more so, perhaps than driving neck and neck in a curricle race or taking part in any of the other wild sports that occupy the time of our young bloods.'

'You were not always a — secret agent,' she said hesitantly. 'Not — when I first met you?'

'No.' His face tightened. 'It was after that. I was looking for something to do that would give my thoughts a new direction. This came in my way, and so —' he shrugged — 'so here I am.'

'And the letter to J. Martin is connected with this,' she said, thoughtfully. 'Yes — I begin to see...'

'I promised to explain and I will. But first I must have your promise that you will not repeat anything I tell you to anyone at all — not your friend, Miss Ellis, nor even your sister Anne, when you next see her. What I am about to reveal to you is not my secret alone, but a secret that is vital to the whole country. Once you've given that undertaking, I know I can rely on you to keep it. Will you give it?'

She promised readily, caught by the gravity of his manner.

'It all started some weeks ago,' he began, leaning forward in his seat to look into her face. 'I managed to bring back to England news of a secret treaty between Boney and Alexander of Russia. Briefly, the result of this treaty would be to place the Danish fleet in French hands, and to give Boney an extra stretch of coastline for an invasion against us.' He broke off, smiling momentarily. 'George Canning is a man of bold ideas, sometimes too bold for some other members of the government. He has his plan, but that plan must be kept a close secret until the last minute. There had to be certain documents drawn up, however, which were placed under lock and key in Mr. Canning's department at the Horse Guards.' He paused. 'That brings us to a certain young man who worked there, and whose name you need not know, for he'll never answer to it again, now.'

Elizabeth drew a quick breath, and looked at him questioningly. He nodded.

'Yes, he's dead — by his own hand, though his death in justice lies at the door of the woman who travelled down in the Mail coach with you from London. She too, is a spy, and her part one that must sicken even someone like myself, used to this treacherous game. She scraped an acquaintance with him

— how, we do not yet know, but such things are simple enough for a good-looking female of determination — and in no time had him eating out of her hand. They are devilish cunning, you know, for he was the weak link in the departmental chain — an inveterate gambler who had run through a private fortune before he joined the Foreign Service, and one with a fondness for the petticoats, into the bargain. They paid him well. No doubt in future there will be some thought given to the hazards of entrusting secret diplomatic papers to those with such tendencies; but there is always a first time for things to go wrong.'

'He stole the papers,' stated Elizabeth, anticipating his next words. 'I suppose that was what was in the packet?'

'Yes, he was ordered to direct them to J. Martin at Crowle Manor, and leave the packet in a coffee house in Whitehall for Mrs. Wood to collect. As you know, it is quite usual for coffee houses to take in letters and packets to be called for. We think that it wasn't originally intended that the woman should take the packet to Lewes herself. The unfortunate young man took longer to lay hands on the documents than the other side had hoped, and this somewhat altered their plans. Afterwards, we found a hastily — and only partly — destroyed letter in a grate at the house where she had been lodging with another woman. From this, we were able to conclude that she'd been instructed at the last minute to take the packet herself to the White Hart at Lewes, and there to deliver it to someone else who would convey it on the last stage of its journey. As far as we could judge from the incomplete letter, the second courier would be unknown to her, and would have to declare himself.'

'And that is exactly what did happen,' said Elizabeth. 'But he declared himself to me, in the beginning, if you remember.'

'Perhaps like myself, he was expecting two females,' replied Farnham. '"One young and personable, the other middle aged" — that was my briefing, and you see how well it fitted yourself and Miss Ellis. Neither of us can be altogether blamed for the error.'

'Hm,' said Elizabeth, doubtfully. 'I would scarcely describe myself in such terms.'

His eyes flicked over her, and came to rest on her face with a look of frank admiration. 'But I would, Elizabeth. Indeed, I have never seen you look lovelier than you do tonight, even when I —' he paused, and took a deep breath — 'even when I was first in love with you.'

She felt herself blushing, and hastened to turn the subject. 'You thought I was the female in the case,' she put in, hurriedly. 'That explains all the things you said that night in my room — I quite thought you had run mad, you know!'

'I must have done, to suspect you of so much evil. Oh, my love, can you ever forgive me?'

'Hush you must not speak so,' she answered, confused so that she could not meet his eyes. 'Of course I forgive you — what else could you think, in the circumstances? But tell me,' she went on, her keen mind still able to worry at the unexplained details of his story, 'how did you find out all this in the first place? If the young man was dead —'

'Not quite, when they found him,' replied Farnham, grimly. 'He told us what he could before the end. I think it was some consolation to him. He was not altogether bad, you know — just foolish.'

She nodded; some of her poise returned now that she had managed to divert his attention from herself.

'But who is J. Martin? And who has the letter — the documents — at present?'

'Potts has them. I overheard this when I was in hiding near the hut. It seems Mrs. Wood succeeded in getting them from your room before I entered it that evening, and she passed them over to the pedlar at once. She left for Brighton the next morning. I have someone watching her, and we shall soon find an opportunity to put her where she can do no more harm. As for the pedlar, he did not come straight to Crowle because my attack on him at the White Hart made him fear someone was on his track. It seems he always takes care not to be seen in company with the smugglers when he's in this part of the country, and when you saw him this morning he was making for a hideaway at the Manor. Seeing you frightened him off.'

'A hideaway here?' Her eyes widened.

He nodded. 'Yes. You have a secret room in this house, Elizabeth — probably a priest's hole from the days when men were obliged to worship in stealth.' She gave a gasp. 'There's an entrance at the side of the house and behind it a staircase that goes up beside the chimney and leads to the attics,' he continued. 'I came in by that way myself just now. It's a small room, connected to the larger one on the other side of it by a false cupboard with a sliding panel at the back. The larger room is full of junk — but perhaps you know?'

Elizabeth shook her head. 'We didn't bother to go up to the attics, as Mrs. Wilmot told us that they were not very tidy, and scarcely worth looking at. She made no mention of this secret room either. Do you suppose that means she is in collusion with that frightful pedlar and the man Martin, whoever he is?'

'Martin, I should think.' He gave the name its French pronunciation.

'He's a spy for the French, and uses the room whenever he's on this side of the Channel; that is, he may have bolt-holes in other places, too, for all I know, but it's his headquarters in this particular area. As for the housekeeper and her husband, I can't say. It seems likely that they know something of what goes on. How else would he get food? And I found some tempting rations up there, stowed away in a real cupboard.'

'Oh, that reminds me!' Elizabeth exclaimed. 'I saw Mrs. Wilmot taking a loaded tray up to the attics earlier this evening. I thought it was strange at the time, but now this explains it, doesn't it! And it means,' she added, 'that she, at any rate, knows what's going on.' She broke off and gave a little shiver. 'All this talk of secret rooms and spies is making me nervous, Robert. Do you mean to tell me that dreadful man Potts is likely to come here at some time, as well as this Frenchman? When? Do you know? Is there nothing you can do to prevent them?'

'They'll be here later tonight.' She gave a violent start, and he leaned over to pat her hand reassuringly. 'You need not worry. There is no reason why they should harm you. The smugglers are expecting a cargo over from France and Martin's coming with it. Around three o'clock, I heard them say. Potts may be here at any time before Martin arrives; he'll hand over the documents and then depart — where, I don't know, but probably off to some other part of the country where he has a similar task to perform. At least, that's what he's planning to do. Our plans for him are somewhat different.' He gave a short, mirthless laugh.

'You say "our plan"?'

'I have helpers — not enough, because I had to send two of them on fruitless errands. One followed Mrs. Wood, as I told you. The other went off to East Bourne on the trail of your friend Miss Ellis. That left me with two. One of them is at this very moment, I hope, riding off to Seaford to fetch military help. The other should be returning here before long, and between us we hope to trap these two miscreants.'

'Miss Ellis? You had Margaret followed?' asked Elizabeth in amazement.

He nodded, looking slightly shamefaced. 'I had to, you know. Although every instinct told me that you must be innocent in this affair —'

'You could not be perfectly sure until you had overheard what Potts had to say about the way in which I came to be in possession of the papers,' she said, taking him up quickly.

'Can you forgive me, Elizabeth?' He looked at her imploringly. 'The first lesson in this business is that one may not trust anybody at all. There can be no exceptions — it's a matter of life and death.'

'Yes, of course I understand that. It seems eminently reasonable.'

He rose from his chair, and, taking her hand before she could guess his intention, carried it to his lips.

'You were always reasonable, my love — a most unfeminine virtue to add to all your other delightfully feminine ones,' he said, raising his head to look down into her eyes.

She blushed, and drew her hand away. 'It is not the time for pretty speeches, Robert. What are you going to do now? You say you have sent for help — will it arrive in time to prevent those two dreadful men from coming to my house?'

'No. That's the last thing I want.' His manner became brisk again. 'If anything should frighten them off from coming here, not only will they slip through my fingers, but I shall most likely lose all chance of recovering the documents. They must be allowed to keep their rendezvous here in the Manor, and we must apprehend them there and then, in the secret room, while they still have the packet on them.'

'But — but that will be dangerous!' protested Elizabeth. 'Suppose the military don't arrive in time, there will only be the two of you to tackle a pair of desperate men! You said yourself that they would stop at nothing!'

'Do you care what happens to me?' he asked, catching her hands in his and pulling her up from her chair, his dark eyes intently fixed upon her face. 'Do you really care, Elizabeth?'

She turned her head away and tried to withdraw her hands from his clasp. 'Of course I do,' she said hurriedly. 'I cannot bear to think of anyone getting hurt — no humane person could — surely?'

'To the devil with such proper sentiments!' he exclaimed impatiently. 'Am I of no more importance to you than the rest of humanity, Elizabeth? You thought differently once, and by heaven I shall make you do so again, before I've done!'

He dropped her hands and seized her impetuously in his arms. She came willingly enough, but he checked suddenly, letting her go and turning away.

'I'm a brute — forgive me, my darling. For a moment, I forgot that you are alone here, to all intents and purposes. It's neither the time nor the place for a declaration — it must wait — I would not force myself upon you. And yet, don't think that I shall let you go so easily this time, Elizabeth. I thought we should never meet again, but now that we have —'

He broke off, seeing her embarrassment, which in truth was acute. He could not know that it was caused not by outraged modesty, as he supposed, but by the sudden realisation that she had not wished him to release her from his embrace, and the hope that she could manage to conceal her feelings for him.

'Enough of that,' he finished, squaring his shoulders. 'I must give you time. And now I'll leave you.'

That brought her to herself quickly. 'But — but what am I to do?' she gasped. 'You can't expect that I shall stay here, with two dangerous men about to enter the house!'

'If I could think of anywhere to take you for refuge believe me I would do it. But there is nowhere close at hand for you to go. I can see no reason why you should not be perfectly safe either in this room, or in your bedchamber, if you prefer it. These men will enter the house by the secret staircase and go nowhere else but to the hidden room above. They will not come into the main part of the house at all — there can be no reason for them to do so. Moreover, in a very short while I myself shall be in the house, concealed in the attic adjoining the priest's hole, waiting to pounce on the pair as soon as Martin arrives. And until then, I shall be watching outside the house until my confederate returns to take over from me.' He broke off, studying her anxious face. 'What about this maid of yours? Is she to be trusted, do you think? Would you like me to summon her to keep you company?'

Elizabeth hesitated. 'I don't know — no, I don't think I want her. She fusses round me too much. I suppose I am being foolish,' she added, reluctantly. 'How I wish I hadn't persuaded Margaret to go away today! However, I must try to be brave — I'm sure any one of my heroines would be!'

'That's my own sweet love,' he said, taking her hands in his. 'Will you stay here or upstairs? In either case, one of us will be quite close at hand to you.'

'I'll stay here,' she answered, forcing a wan smile 'You — you'll take care, Robert? I'm so afraid for you — '

'Never fear, love,' he carried her hand to his lips. 'I have everything now to induce me to take care of myself.'

He turned away to retrieve his lantern, which he had earlier placed on the floor.

'Fasten the window after me, dearest,' he said, as he opened it and dropped lightly out on to the ground beneath.

Chapter XVIII: The Best Laid Schemes

After Claudette Faubourg had returned to her room, she suddenly realised that the noise she had heard could not, after all, have been caused by the cat. She was not herself a cat lover, but the housekeeper was; and Claudette distinctly remembered Mrs. Wilmot complaining just before she retired for the night that her precious Timmy had not returned from his usual nocturnal expedition.

'Taken up with some female in the village again, I suppose,' the housekeeper had remarked, with a sniff. 'Oh, well, it's human nature as well as cat nature, I dare say, but it's to be hoped my precious don't get into any fights, for he's a real beauty, and I can't abear the thought of him coming back all battered, poor little thing!'

And if he had since come back, reflected Claudette, he certainly could not have found a way in, with every window shut and all the doors bolted. From what she knew of the animal, he would be far more likely to set up a yowling under the housekeeper's window, too, rather than seek an entrance for himself.

So it was not the cat. Then who was it? An expected or an unexpected visitor? It was extremely unlikely to be the former, all things considered. She had better make sure.

In spite of the fact that she had been sent off to bed over an hour ago, she was still fully dressed.

She set her candle down, and tiptoed to the door, straining her ears for the sound of any movement from outside. None came, and after a while she cautiously opened the door and peered out.

She was just in time to catch sight of a glimmer of light that was moving down the attic staircase.

She stayed where she was, watching its progress. At the foot of the stairs, it halted for a moment, changing position as someone evidently raised it higher to see ahead. She caught a brief glimpse of a dark shape behind it, and then it once more returned to its former position and vanished from sight, presumably as its bearer turned along the passage towards the main staircase.

Someone was prowling round the house.

She waited to see if the prowler would return, but nothing happened. He must have gone downstairs. She wondered if Miss Thorne was still in the parlour, or if she had come upstairs to bed. Perhaps it would be as well to find out. She started to turn back into her room to pick up the candle, then changed her mind. She could find her way round the house without a light, and it would be safer to do so. She left the candle burning, closed the door quietly, and carefully went down to Miss Thorne's bedchamber on the next floor.

A fire had been left in the grate, for the evening was chilly. It was not quite burnt out; the red embers relieved the gloom sufficiently for her to see her way about. She moved over to the bed, which was undisturbed. Miss Thorne was downstairs, then, no doubt still hard at work on her writing. Perhaps the prowler would walk in on her; if so there would be a scream presently to break the silence of the house. She thought of the Wilmots, safely tucked up in bed, and her lips twisted in contempt. They had locked themselves in and declared that nothing would fetch them out until daylight appeared. Craven fools! They were ready enough to take the pickings, so long as they did not become too deeply involved. But if anything went wrong, there would be no more pickings, for them or for anyone else. All the same, she knew it would be useless to try to rouse them and ask for Wilmot's help. Although properly speaking this was man's work, she must tackle it herself. She left Elizabeth's room and, treading cautiously, made her way slowly down the main staircase.

A lamp was still burning in the hall, so she halted before she reached the foot of the stairs, leaning over the balustrade to see if anyone was about. Suddenly the door of the back parlour opened, and a man emerged. She drew her head back quickly, crouching on the stairs and peering through the openings in the balustrade. If he came this way, she was cornered and must brazen things out as best she could. After all, she was Miss Thorne's maid, and could be on an errand for her mistress. But who was he? Was he the prowler whom she had been following? If so, why had not Miss Thorne screamed for help when he had entered the parlour?

The man did not come any farther, but looked about him keenly, then went back into the room and closed the door. Claudette let out a long-drawn breath. She was not quite sure what to do next, but she felt certain that she ought to try and find out who this man was who had entered the room where Miss Thorne was sitting. Miss Thorne could not have called for help, or Claudette would have been bound to hear her. That must mean either that she had fainted or been overpowered by the man, or else that she had not been at all alarmed because she already knew him.

Claudette Faubourg's face was a grim one at best, but it became more grim as this thought crossed her mind. She had been employed by several ladies in high society, and knew something of 'goings-on', as she termed them; but Miss Elizabeth Thorne had not struck her as the kind of female to meet a man clandestinely. One could never tell, of course;

sometimes it was those who seemed most demure who were capable of the most scandalous behaviour. But she could think of no reason for Miss Thorne to meet a lover in secret down here in Crowle, where there was no one to know or care about her personal affairs. The only person who might have been supposed to take an interest was Miss Ellis, and she had left the house that afternoon. Why, then, this secrecy?

She must find out. Any unexpected arrival on the scene at this particular time was a potential hazard to what was afoot. If the man and Miss Thorne were known to each other, and were even now talking together in the parlour, then it might be possible to overhear something of their conversation through the keyhole of the door. Great care would be necessary; the man had come out of the room once to look around, and might do so again. Perhaps it would be safer to try and listen at the inner door of the ante-room; he was less likely to go that way to the passage. And if she were caught, she had always the excuse that she had come in search of her mistress, finding that Miss Thorne was not yet in her bedchamber.

Having made up her mind, she crept cautiously down the rest of the stairs and tiptoed across the intervening space to the door of the ante-room. She went slowly, trying to remember which of the floorboards were liable to creak. Her pulse beat increased a fraction as she passed the parlour door, but she did not falter, for she had a cool head and was not unused to exploits of this kind.

She reached her objective without incident, and softly turned the knob on the other side without allowing it to give a betraying click. Then she sidled into the room, closing the door gently behind her. So far, so good. She paused a moment to give herself a breathing space before she trod quietly across the small room to the door which communicated with the parlour.

Now she could hear the low murmur of voices from the room beyond.

So these two were known to each other, as she had suspected; but was it merely a clandestine love affair, or something more sinister?

She squinted through the keyhole though without very much hope of seeing what was going on, for she knew from past experience that people were rarely so obliging as to station themselves in direct line with the door. She soon gave up the attempt, and applied her ear to the keyhole, listening intently.

At first, she found this scarcely more rewarding. It was easy enough to recognise Miss Thorne's pleasant voice, and to hear the deeper tones of the man's. To distinguish any words, however, was much more difficult, as they were both speaking in lowered voices. After a time, her ear became more accustomed, and she found herself able to pick out a phrase or two here and there in the conversation.

What she heard was of sufficient interest to keep her at the keyhole. The man seemed to be doing most of the talking. She heard him say that he was a spy, and caught the mention of Jean Martin's name. He appeared to be giving Miss Thorne an account of events in which she had unwittingly been involved in a small way. Here Claudette found little difficulty in supplementing what she managed to hear; she knew the facts well enough. But when he went on to speak of the secret room and of the plans he had made for the capture of Potts and Jean, she was tormented by the inadequacy of the information she was able to obtain. Only two of them — had she heard aright? One would be watching outside, the other hiding in the attic. She smiled grimly. Well, Jean was more than a match for any two other men, while Potts, too, was a formidable enough opponent.

All the same, they must be warned what to expect. The man was going now — she had heard him say earlier that he must leave, but there was still some nonsense going on between him and the female. Evidently the two were lovers. Perhaps that fact might prove useful. Claudette's mind ranged swiftly over possible courses of action. Could she slip out of the house unobserved to warn Potts? It seemed scarcely likely, as one of these men would be watching outside all the time, by what she had heard. Besides, she was not at all sure where Potts might be found at present, and a great deal of time could be wasted in running him to earth. One thing she did know for certain was that he would be coming here before long. It was usual for him to arrive an hour or so before Jean.

She nodded sagely to herself. She would leave it to Potts. He would know what to do.

She straightened up, arching her cramped back and massaging her neck. The room beyond had been silent since she had heard only a few minutes ago the faint sound of a window closing. Evidently the man had left by that exit, and Miss Thorne was now alone. It would be a good moment for her to go too. She turned on her heel, intending to tiptoe quietly from the room; but her recent stooping had momentarily upset her sense of balance, so that she stumbled against the door.

She drew back quickly, putting her hands to her mouth in alarm.

She was still in this attitude when the door was thrust open and Elizabeth Thorne faced her accusingly.

'Claudette!' she exclaimed. 'What are you doing here?'

'I — I was just coming to see if you were all right, madam. I thought I heard a noise as if someone was prowling round the house,' replied Claudette, glibly.

Elizabeth looked unconvinced. 'If that is so, why are you standing here in the dark? If you were anxious about me, I should have thought it more natural to rush into the room at once.'

Claudette thought quickly. 'I was about to, madam, but then I thought I heard voices, and scarcely liked to intrude if you were talking to someone.'

'Voices! How long have you been here, Claudette? Answer me at once — and truthfully, mind.'

'Only a few minutes.' Claudette bridled. 'And as to answering truthfully, madam, I'm sure I've never been accused of lying before — me, who's served in some of the best families in the land!'

Elizabeth stared at her thoughtfully. 'Yes,' she said, slowly, 'perhaps you are telling the truth. But all the same, I can't afford to take the risk.'

She turned away without another word and started across the room towards the window.

Claudette leapt forward and seized her arm. 'What are you going to do?'

'That's no concern of yours,' replied Elizabeth, coldly. 'Let me go.'

'So that you can let your lover know I've been listening to his little schemes? Oh, no, my fine lady!'

Claudette clamped a strong arm about Elizabeth, and covered her mouth with relentless fingers. Elizabeth had not expected it, and found herself at a decided disadvantage in the short struggle which followed. Her adversary was no taller than she was, but was undoubtedly both stronger and heavier. She managed to wrench one arm free, and tore desperately at the hand which was fastened over her mouth, but without avail.

She writhed and kicked but in spite of her struggles, Claudette was gradually pushing her down towards the floor.

They were near to the writing-desk where Elizabeth's manuscript lay as she had left it, with a large metal paperweight on top. Suddenly she remembered the paperweight. She stopped trying to move Claudette's hand from her mouth, and instead made a violent lunge towards the desk, her fingers groping for the weapon.

The quick-witted Claudette guessed her intention, and put every ounce of strength into dragging her away from the desk. They swayed and lost balance. Elizabeth fell, striking her head on the corner of the desk, and dragging Claudette down to the floor with her. The weight of the abigail would have driven the breath from Elizabeth's body had she not already been senseless from the blow on her head.

Chapter XIX: Baiting the Trap

The village of Crowle was shrouded in darkness, as might have been expected at past one o'clock in the morning. Yet there were furtive signs of life stirring. Dark figures crept from almost every cottage; at the back of the Martlet Inn a horse with padded hoofs was being harnessed to a cart with cloth twisted about the wheel rims, while ponies from nearby farms stood by patiently, waiting as if they understood what they would shortly be expected to do.

At Crowle Manor, the hitherto quiet stables showed similar stealthy signs of movement. The horses that were led out also had padded hoofs; in spite of this Farnham, uneasily keeping a prolonged vigil in the unaccountable absence of his lieutenant, heard them moving along the drive and guessed where they were bound, and why the familiar beat of hoofs was missing.

He wondered what the devil his man Denning could be doing; he should have been here long since. Without him, it would be difficult if not impossible to take Potts and the spy Martin into custody; and there could be no certainty that the military would arrive in time. He had hoped to be inside the house before this, near to Elizabeth. She had tried to put a brave face on things, but he knew how very nervous she felt. Her alarm was natural enough, but he could not seriously feel that she had anything to fear. All the same, he would prefer to be within reach of her; but it was out of the question to desert his post here until Denning arrived to relieve him.

As these uneasy thoughts crossed his mind, he caught the faint sound of a twig snapping under foot from the trees behind. This must be his man at last. He waited for the owl's cry that was their arranged signal.

It did not come. He was about to give it himself, when some extra sense warned him against it. He was standing in the shelter of some bushes which overlooked the entrance to the secret passage. He remained where he was, motionless, listening intently.

No other sound followed the first, which he now began to think must have been made by some animal on its nocturnal maraudings. He was about to move so as to ease his tensed muscles, when he heard close at hand the soft padding of footsteps, and a moment later, a dark shadow brushed past his hiding place and moved stealthily towards the hidden door.

He knew then that this could not be Denning and was thankful that he had refrained from giving the signal. Was it Potts or the Frenchman? It was impossible to identify anyone on a moonless night such as this, but the odds were that it was Potts.

With eyes accustomed to the darkness, Farnham watched the shadowy figure pause a moment before the secret door, then vanish quickly from sight. He resisted an urge to look at his watch. The last time he had done so, it had been a little after one; that must have been half an hour or more since. Denning had been gone two hours on an errand that should have taken him half an hour at most. Something must have gone wrong.

He made a quick reassessment of his plans. Only an incurable optimist could suppose that one man could capture single-handed two desperate villains like Potts and Martin. From the first, he had been concerned to plan matters so that both men should be safely in the secret room before any attempt upon them was made. Now it looked as if the only possibility of success lay in tackling one at a time. If Martin should in some way be scared off by this means, it was a hazard that must be faced. By far the most important thing was to recover the documents, and Potts was the man who had them in his possession.

All the same, he was reluctant to abandon his original scheme just yet. Feeling it safe to do so now that Potts had been gone for some minutes, he consulted his watch briefly by a tiny gleam from the lantern. It was ten minutes to two. He had heard the men at the hut say that the smugglers could not be expected much before three o'clock, and the spy Martin had to make his way here from the beach after landing. He could surely afford to wait until half past two for Denning to appear.

Elizabeth stirred, becoming conscious of something tied about her mouth in an acutely uncomfortable way. She tried to raise her hands to deal with this, only to find that they were firmly tied, too; and behind her back, so that she could not bring them to her assistance.

It took a few moments for her to realise where she was and what had befallen her. Then she recalled the struggle with Claudette and hitting her head on the desk as the abigail forced her to the floor. She was still lying there, she discovered; the place on her head felt sore, her limbs were cramped and the gag was cutting into her mouth. It must have been Claudette who had secured her in this fashion to prevent her from warning Robert that the abigail had overheard their conversation. If she could only lay her hands on the minx! But much good it would do her, she reflected ruefully, a moment afterwards, for in the recent tussle she had seen only too clearly who held the advantage.

Robert! A warning bell clanged in her still hazy mind. He had hoped to trap Potts and the spy in the secret room, but now

Claudette knew this, the trap would become an ambush for the King's men. Somehow she must reach Robert and warn him that his raid would be expected.

She tried to move, emitting a choked groan at the effort. A second attempt brought the welcome discovery that her feet had not been tied. She was lying on the floor not far from the desk which had caused her injury. If she could manoeuvre herself against this it might be possible to work herself into a sitting position, and from thence to her feet.

She was about to make an attempt to put this plan into action, when she heard the door opening. Thinking it safer to feign unconsciousness for the moment, she closed her eyes.

She heard two people come into the room, and a moment later, one of them was bending over her. She knew it was Claudette, for the abigail's voice sounded close to her.

'She's still unconscious. *Nom de Dieu*, I hope I haven't killed her!'

'Fustian! 'Tis only a swoon.' She felt herself turned over, and rough hands explored her hair, looking for the injury that had knocked her out. With real heroism, she suppressed a wince as Potts — for she recognised his voice immediately — found it. 'See, it's not even broken the skin,' he continued, displaying a large bruise at the back of Elizabeth's head. 'It's wonder it's kept her out for so long, but female's is delicate things. Still, it's as well you didn't kill her, for though it may come to that in the end, that's for Monsoor Martin to say. He don't like anything o' that nature bein' done without his orders, as ye'll soon learn, even if ye don' know now.'

Claudette sprang to her feet. 'You think you can tell me anything about my *cher* cousin Jean, you?' she asked scornfully. 'You others — the hen-witted female who calls herself Mrs. Wood who kept house with me in London, and you who carry messages for one and another — you can never know him as I do! Certainly he does not like anyone to be killed near to his hiding places, for a corpse draws attention, and that is something he does not seek. But I do not see how we can keep this female alive,' she finished, in a ruminative tone. 'She knows too much, and in a few days her female companion will be returning. And Jean will be forced to wait here for a day or so before he can get a passage back to France.'

'You said these two are lovers, the secret agent and this female,' put in Potts. 'It all depends what Monsoor Martin thinks o' course but seems to me if we could make it look as though they'd run away together —'

Claudette laughed. 'Excellent! My friend, you are not so stupid as you appear. But first we must catch the man, and that may not be so easy. As I told you, there are two of them —'

'Not now,' replied Potts, chuckling. 'Someone was nosing around the hut while Reuben and me was there. On the way back to the village, we comes on a horseman riding along. Rueben reckons it won't be any o' his lot so we gives chase. A fine dance he leads us, but we caught him at last and pops him a few questions. He tells some rigmarole about losing his road and wanting to get to East Bourne, that wouldn't have deceived a babe in arms. We was in two minds to slit his throat there an' then, but thinks better of it because of Monsoor Martin, so we knocks him on the 'ead and flings 'im into the cellar at the "Martlet", where he's likely getting himself drunk this very minute, if he's any sense. But Rueben swears he was the same man as came round seekin' a bed in the village a couple o' days back, so there's no doubt he's the partner to this agent o' yourn.'

'Very likely, but all the same he's not the man who was watching you when you were in the hut. That was this other man — the one she calls Robert.' She aimed a kick at the seemingly unconscious Elizabeth. 'How I despise her! All the time she thought I was dancing attendance on her, she never seemed to guess that my real object was to make sure she didn't find out too much. But they are stupid, the English — they trust people.'

'Not if they're in business, they don't. But how d'ye know that it was this Robert fellow who was round the hut, and not t'other one?'

'I heard him tell her so. I couldn't hear all he said, more's the pity, but that part was clear enough. So was the plan to take you and Jean in the priest's hole — one man was to hide in the attic, the other to follow up the secret staircase after you were both seen to enter.'

'Ye're certain there was no more than two of 'em?' insisted Potts.

'Quite certain. I remember Miss Thorne saying how alarmed she was at the thought of there being only two of them to tackle two such desperate characters as you and Jean.'

'Ye're positive this man Robert's not in the house now?'

She hesitated. 'Not positive, but I heard him say that he intended to wait outside until the other man returned. Then he went out through this window.'

'He'll have a long wait, if so. But I'll just take a look upstairs to make sure. You stay here with madam.'

Elizabeth's heart sank as she heard this. It put an end to all her hopes of being able to free herself, and moreover she did not know how much longer she could feign unconsciousness. Now that there was nothing else to take her attention, Claudette would not readily be deceived.

But the abigail, after one contemptuous glance at the recumbent form of her mistress, turned her attention to the writing-desk. She removed the paperweight from the folder which contained Elizabeth's manuscript, and taking out some of the pages, started to read them.

Elizabeth raged inwardly. To have her most cherished and private possessions violated by the glance of this creature hurt her far more than any of the indignities she has so far suffered. In her indignation she could lie still no longer, and gave a violent lurch towards the desk.

Claudette looked up. 'So you've come to, madam, have you?' she said, with a sneer. 'Well, better for you if you hadn't, as you'll soon find.'

She dropped the papers and came to stand over Elizabeth, taunting her with all the pent-up malice which years of unwilling servitude had endangered in her. Elizabeth soon learned that the abigail's employment in certain high households had been a means to the end of obtaining information for the French, and not a matter of choice. She listened in shocked surprise while the stream of vituperation poured out of the woman; it was her first experience of a bitter hatred such as this, and she found it terrifying.

After a few minutes she managed to get her fear under control sufficiently to wonder if she could not turn the other woman's emotional state to good account. But what could she do, handicapped as she was? The answer came to her in a flash and she acted upon it.

Suddenly she drew up her legs and kicked out at Claudette with all the force she could muster.

The woman staggered, clutched at the air, and fell at Elizabeth's side.

At once Elizabeth rolled over on top of her, hoping that the sudden weight would deprive her of her senses for long enough for Elizabeth to try and free herself.

It was a gallant attempt that could have small chance of success. Claudette was both heavier and stronger than her opponent, besides being free. She had flung Elizabeth from her and was starting to her feet to begin reprisals when Potts came into the room.

'What the devil —?' he began, seizing Claudette's arm as she was about to aim a blow at Elizabeth. 'What's going on here?'

'This hell cat!' panted the abigail. 'She kicked me over, by God, she'll pay for it!'

He gave her a shake. 'Never mind about that now — there's no time for it. Ye'll get yer own back soon, never fear. Now, listen. Yon cove isn't up there yet, but I reckon he soon will be, when he gets fed up o' waitin' for his pal. So we'll fix a little trap up for 'im, see, and this young lady 'ere can bait it.'

'What do you mean?'

'Why, he'll come up the stairs and into the secret room, won't he? And if I'm there waitin', we'll make a fight o' it, and likely I'll get in first. But just to make sure, we could put something there that'll draw 'is attention away from everything else, couldn't we? Then I can take 'im easy, and by surprise.'

'You mean her?'

'What else? Now, just you take the candle and show madam up to her bedchamber.'

He gave a chuckle, and, bending over Elizabeth, tossed her up over his shoulder as easily as though she had been a sack of vegetables. She tried to kick, but he clamped her legs firmly with one arm as he made for the door.

Effortlessly, he carried her up the two flights of stairs to the attic, then stood aside for Claudette to open the secret door. They entered the hidden room and he threw Elizabeth roughly on the narrow bed.

'Lie there, my pretty ladybird, till yer lover comes to ye,' he said, mockingly.

Then he turned to Claudette, who was advancing threateningly on her mistress.

'As for ye — out.' He pointed to the door which led into the attic.

She looked rebellious for a moment, then obeyed. He followed her out, carefully closing the outer door of the cupboard, but not the panel behind it, which led into the attic.

Left alone, Elizabeth tried desperately to think of something — anything — that could save Robert from the ambush that awaited him.

Chapter XX: The End of a Secret Agent

Farnham looked at his watch again. It was five and twenty to three. Reluctantly he decided that he could not afford to wait any longer for Denning. Something serious must have happened to delay him all this time; his help could no longer be counted upon. Any further delay would chance the arrival of Martin on the scene, and then there would be two men to deal with instead of one.

He fastened the lantern to his belt, looked to the priming of his pistol and holding it in his left hand, glided through the shadows to the secret door. His fingers found the catch and he stepped inside, shutting the door behind him. Relying on memory and his sense of touch, he cautiously ascended the stairs until he came to the second sliding panel. Then he went back a few steps, until by bending forward he could just reach the catch. As the door slid open, he ducked his head and waited.

Nothing happened, although he could see that there was a light in the room. Transferring his pistol to his right hand, he cocked it and pointed it into the room, cautiously raising his head a little so that he could see inside.

The light came from a lantern hanging on the wall over the bed; it was shining full on a recumbent form which lay there. Farnham took one look at the tumbled brown locks and dishevelled blue gown trailing over the bed and on to the floor, and his heart turned over. Then he leapt forward, reaching Elizabeth's side in one bound.

'My darling! In God's name, what's happened to you?'

She had only one way to warn him, and that was with her eyes. She darted a fearful glance at the cupboard, and he understood at once. Keeping his pistol trained in that direction, he moved so that he was half-facing towards her and half towards the danger.

'Whoever did this to you, my love, they shall pay for it!' he said between clenched teeth. 'Turn towards the wall, and I'll soon get you free.'

She rolled over, and he worked at the knot that secured the gag over her mouth. He was almost as adept with his left hand as with his right, and in a few seconds his strong fingers had untied it. He pulled the cloth gently away from her mouth, then swore as he saw the red marks left by its pressure.

With another quick glance towards the cupboard, he began to untie her hands. He had just succeeded in working the knot free when the cupboard door was flung open.

He leapt to his feet, standing in front of Elizabeth to shield her, and pointed his pistol at the cupboard, ready to shoot.

No one appeared in the aperture, but a harsh voice came from behind the open door.

'Lay down yer pistol, or I'll shoot the pair o' ye.'

Farnham made no answer, but signalled to Elizabeth to crawl under the bed. She understood at once, but had some difficulty in obeying because of the stiffness in her arms after being bound. He dared not help her, but kept his eyes unflinchingly on the aperture between the two rooms, ready to shoot as soon as Potts showed any part of his body, as he must do before he could take aim with his pistol.

Evidently Potts had no mind to do this, and for the moment it was a stalemate. Meanwhile Elizabeth tumbled in a heap on to the floor behind Farnham, and painfully crawled underneath the bed.

Nothing happened for several minutes. Elizabeth was massaging her numbed wrists, while Farnham contemplated making a charge into the adjoining room.

All at once Potts thrust his head round the door and fired his pistol.

Farnham flung himself flat, at the same time firing his own weapon. The ball from the pedlar's pistol whistled harmlessly over Farnham's head, embedding itself in the wall; while Farnham had no better luck, as his target had appeared too briefly for his purpose. He did not pause to reload but cast the pistol aside and leapt through the opening into the adjoining room, chancing that Potts might have a second pistol ready to discharge at him.

Fortune was with him. The pedlar was just about to reload his pistol as Farnham jumped upon him, knocking it out of his grasp. The two men were soon locked together in a grim struggle, while Claudette stood, helplessly by, screaming vituperation.

Elizabeth listened anxiously, and debated with herself whether there was anything she could do to help. Some of the use was returning now to her hands, and although her mouth felt sore and her throat dry and parched she was beyond caring about anything but what was happening to Robert. Suddenly she realised how much he still meant to her; and that life would no longer hold anything that mattered if they were to be parted again.

She had almost made up her mind to venture out of her hiding place, when she thought she heard a faint sound from the panel which gave access to the secret staircase. It was difficult to be sure with all the noise that was coming from the attic; she strained her ears, trying to shut out the sounds of conflict. She had almost decided that she had imagined it, when a pair of boots came into her line of vision crossing the floor past her hiding place. At the same moment, a sudden hush fell in the attic, until Claudette's voice was heard once more, screaming and ranting.

Elizabeth's heart stood still. There was someone else in the room, approaching the attic with stealthy tread. Who could it be? The man whom Robert had expected to come to his aid, or that other, the spy Martin? And what did the sudden silence from the other room portend? Did it mean that one of the men had laid out the other? Pray heaven that it might not be Robert who had been defeated! She *must* do something — but what was best to do?

She was beginning to creep quietly out from under the bed, when she heard an unfamiliar voice speaking from the open cupboard into the room beyond. She peered out, and saw a short, squarely-built man in fisherman's garb standing inside the cupboard with his back to her, facing into the attic. His right arm was raised in a threatening attitude; it held a pistol.

'Put up your hands!' he snarled.

Elizabeth heard Claudette scream, 'Jean!' She knew then without a doubt who it was.

'What goes on here?' rapped out Jean Martin. 'Tell me at once, Claudette, and don't be long about it.'

Claudette burst into a torrent of French which was too fast for Elizabeth to follow with any certainty; but it did seem that Robert had succeeded in knocking out Potts just as Martin had arrived on the scene.

'So this is an English agent,' said Martin, when he had listened to Claudette's story for a few minutes. 'He will not trouble us for long. Someone shall take you for a short trip on the sea, my friend, but there'll be no return passage. Claudette, find some strong cord to truss up this man, and be quick about it.'

Elizabeth heard Claudette's footsteps as the abigail went off to obey this command. She realised that now, if at any time, she must do something to help Robert. The cupboard door stood open, offering the only cover in the room, and the head of the bed was behind it. She wriggled out at this point, careful to make no sound, and pulled herself to her feet against the wall. As she did so, her eye fell on Farnham's pistol which he had cast aside when he had rushed into the attic. Quietly she stooped to retrieve it. She had no notion how to load a pistol, even if the powder and ball had been to hand; but at least, she thought pugnaciously, grasping it by the muzzle, she might manage to stun Martin with it. The only thing that worried her was that the attempt might cause him to let off his own weapon at Robert.

She realised this was no time for doubts and fears. At any moment Claudette would return with the cord, and once Robert was bound hand and foot, he could do nothing to help himself. If she could only give him a chance, however slender, she knew he was opportunist enough to benefit from it.

She crept round the cupboard door, the weapon raised in her hand. Farnham saw her, and a keen look came into his eyes. Either it was this, or she must have made some slight sound, for suddenly Martin turned towards her. She shrank back retreating against the bed.

In a flash, Farnham was on him and had knocked the pistol from his hand. It went spinning across the floor towards the panel which concealed the staircase, discharging itself with a roar.

Elizabeth let out an involuntary scream before she managed to control herself and sink, shaking, on to the bed. Claudette came running into the attic shouting to know what was amiss. The two men were engaged in a desperate struggle on the floor. For a moment, it looked as if Claudette meant to launch herself into the fray; but she thought better of it, and contented herself with leaning against the wall and screaming encouragement to the Frenchman.

Elizabeth looked on in horror while the two men wrestled fiercely for mastery. If only there were anything she could do! But first one was on top, then the other; and even if she attempted to club Martin with the pistol she was still grasping, she might quite likely hit the wrong man.

Her nerves were almost at breaking point when a thunderous knocking sounded throughout the house. Stentorian voices accompanied it: 'In the King's name! Open, in the King's name!'

The combatants paused; Claudette ceased to shout. And clearly from outside the house could be heard the pounding of hoofs, jingling of harness and the tramping of spurred boots.

'The dragoons!' panted Farnham. 'Praise be!'

Martin began to struggle like a fiend, but Farnham held him fast. Suddenly Elizabeth knew what she could do. Seizing the lantern from over the bed, she rushed from the room, through the attic, down the two flights of stairs and to the front door. She drew back the bolts with hands that trembled, admitting two officers and several men who were standing on the step.

'Thank God you are here!' she gasped. 'Come quickly!'

It was several hours later. Elizabeth was reflecting, not without a certain relish, that it really was most improper to be travelling in a coach all alone with a gentleman in the early hours of the morning, even if that coach happened to be accompanied by a military escort.

'Poor Margaret!' she exclaimed to her companion. 'She will have a sad shock, seeing me on the doorstep at this hour, and quite unannounced. It is to be hoped Cousin Ernestine will not be put about.'

'From what I know of Miss Ellis, she will make no to do about that,' he replied, squeezing her hand, which had somehow slipped into his. 'Anyway, it won't be for long. I must go to London post haste now to deliver these papers, but I'll be back to claim my bride before the week is out.'

'Oh, Robert!' she protested, with a blush. 'As if I could marry you as quickly as that!'

'Why not? There's no need for delay that I can see — God knows we've waited long enough already. Do you propose we should wait another six years?'

He put his fingers under her chin and tilted it up so that he could look into her eyes.

'Don't be absurd,' she answered, with a smile. 'But Anne would never forgive me if —'

'We're not consulting Anne's wishes, now or in the future,' he warned her. 'She's had her run, and a good long run for it. Now it's my turn. I warn you, dearest, I mean to monopolise you shamefully.'

She murmured that she would have no complaint about this, and for a time there was silence in the coach. Presently Elizabeth protested, and tried to straighten her tumbled hair.

'Dearest, you will be careful when you take these documents to London, won't you?' she begged anxiously.

'I shall have a full military escort. Have no fear.'

'There's one thing,' she went on, hesitantly. 'I don't think — Robert, are you so very determined to remain a secret agent? Only I would much prefer you not to — but, of course, I don't wish to stand in the way of anything you really want to do.'

'Spoken like a good dutiful wife,' he laughed, then sobered again. 'No, I think perhaps it's not an occupation for a married man. I shall apply myself to other pursuits for the future — buy a house in the country, settle down, rear a family — how will that suit you, eh?'

She gave a sigh of deep contentment, settling herself comfortably in the warm shelter of his encircling arm.

Acknowledgements

The author would like to thank the Records department of the G.P.O for supplying information about mail coaches in the early nineteenth century; also Mrs. George Bambridge for permission to reprint the lines from Rudyard Kipling's poem 'A Smuggler's Song'.

A NOTE TO THE READER

It's wonderful to see my mother's books available again and being enjoyed by what must surely be a new audience from that which read them when they were first published. My brother and I can well remember our mum, Alice, writing away on her novels in the room we called the library at home when we were teenagers. She generally laid aside her pen — there were no computers in those days, of course — when we returned from school but we knew she had used our absence during the day to polish off a few chapters.

One of the things I well remember from those days is the care that she took in ensuring the historical accuracy of the background of her books. I am sure many of you have read novels where you are drawn out of the story by inaccuracies in historical facts, details of costume or other anachronisms. I suppose it would be impossible to claim that there are no such errors in our mother's books; what is undoubted is that she took great care to check matters.

The result was, and is, that the books still have an appeal to a modern audience, for authenticity is appreciated by most readers, even if subconsciously. The periods in which they set vary: the earliest is *The Georgian Rake*, which must be around the middle of the 18th century; and some are true Regency romances. But Mum was not content with just a love story; there is always an element of mystery in her books. Indeed, this came to the fore in her later writings, which are historical detective novels.

There's a great deal more I could say about her writings but it would be merely repeating what you can read on her website at **www.alicechetwyndley.co.uk**. To outward appearances, our mother was an average housewife of the time — for it was usual enough for women to remain at home in those days — but she possessed a powerful imagination that enabled her to dream up stories that appealed to many readers at the time — and still do, thanks to their recent republication.

If you have enjoyed her novels, we would be very grateful if you could leave a review on **Amazon** or **Goodreads** so that others may also be tempted to lose themselves in their pages.

Richard Ley, 2018.

Sapere Books is an exciting new publisher of brilliant fiction and popular history.

To find out more about our latest releases and our monthly bargain books visit our website:
saperebooks.com

17540636R00116

Printed in Great Britain
by Amazon